# Stained Glass Window

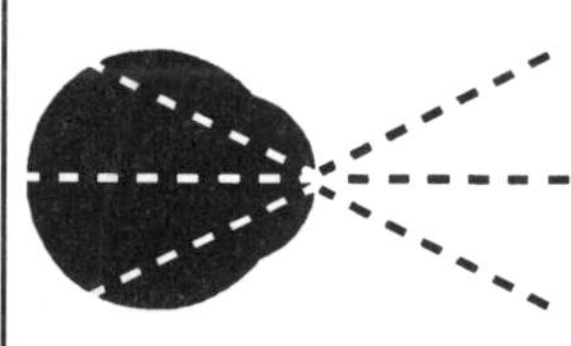

This Large Print Book carries the Seal of Approval of N.A.V.H.

# STAINED GLASS WINDOW

INNIS GRACE

**THORNDIKE PRESS**
*An imprint of Thomson Gale, a part of The Thomson Corporation*

Detroit • New York • San Francisco • New Haven, Conn. • Waterville, Maine • London

Thorndike Press, an imprint of The Gale Group.


This novel is a work of fiction. Names, characters, places, and incidents are either the product of the author's imagination, or, if real, used fictitiously.

Thorndike Press® Large Print Clean Reads.
The text of this Large Print edition is unabridged.
Other aspects of the book may vary from the original edition.
Set in 16 pt. Plantin.

**LIBRARY OF CONGRESS CATALOGING-IN-PUBLICATION DATA**

Grace, Innis, 1952–
Stained glass window / by Innis Grace.
p. cm. — (Thorndike Press large print clean reads)
ISBN-13: 978-0-7862-9754-2 (lg. print : alk. paper)
ISBN-10: 0-7862-9754-9 (lg. print : alk. paper)
1. Marital conflict — Fiction. 2. Separated people — Fiction. 3. Glass painting and staining — Fiction. 4. Diaries — Fiction. 5. Reconciliation — Fiction. 6. Large type books. I. Title.
PS3553.A81433S73 2007
813'.6—dc22 2007017842

Published in 2007 by arrangement with Tekno Books and Ed Gorman.

Printed in the United States of America on permanent paper
10 9 8 7 6 5 4 3 2 1

For the Lord and those who love me.

# ONE

*Tear Lake, Colorado. April 2004*

It was a lovely, warm spring night when the phone on Leigh's bed stand rang. Phil was due home anytime and she thought it might be him as she picked up the phone and said, "Hello."

"Is this Leigh?" an unfamiliar man's voice asked.

"Yes."

"Are you still married to Phillip?"

"Yes — what is this about —" Her heart thudded hard and a little voice in her head said, *You know what it is about. You have been in denial, but you know.*

"Look, I hate to be the one to tell you this, but your husband is having an affair."

"That is ridiculous. How could you know such a thing?"

"Because he is having the affair with my wife."

Leigh woke from the nightmare with her

throat burning and tears still wet on her face. The sheet was tangled around her body and her heart was pumping like a piston. Would she ever be able to close her eyes without having that moment creep into her dreams? She had paced the floor that night, waited for Phillip, hoping he would deny it all. But he hadn't. He had hung his head in shame and admitted that he had been pursuing a woman.

"A younger woman." That hated voice of her own pain reminded her.

Phillip, her knight in shining armor, the father of her child, didn't even have the creativity to be original. He was a forty-something married man cheating with a younger woman. "How clichéd," that voice pointed out.

Her anger had been a palpable thing, writhing just beneath the surface. Leigh had always prided herself on her ability to remain calm. For the first time in her life she had broken something in a rage. The vase Phil had given her on their last anniversary had shattered not far from his head. Too bad her aim hadn't been better. But that emotional outburst, so foreign to her, had only been the beginning. She had gone on a rampage, packing away his pictures in the basement, sending his easy chair to charity, canceling his favorite magazines — after she had packed his clothes and set them neatly in the driveway. She never knew if he went to a hotel or straight into the woman's arms when she told him to leave that night.

Now Leigh was at her grandmother's old house, high in the mountains, hiding from her own failed marriage, trying to escape the person she had seen in the mirror the day she had gone crazy, because she had been a little out of her mind — and very out of control. That nearly mad woman had hurt in her eyes, but she also had something else — something wild and primitive in her heart, something waiting to be unleashed. That unknown reflection that had stared back from the mirror had scared Leigh into a moment of sanity and clarity. So she was trying to get her head on straight here in Tear Lake, calm, isolated and far away from Phillip and his mid-life crisis.

"The jerk," she said aloud. Because even though she was finding her center again, she was still furious and hurt.

Suddenly all those women, the ones she had never understood, the ones that ended up in the newspaper because they had blown up their husband's car, or run down the philanderer in a motel parking lot, or hired a private detective to take photos, were her sisters-in-craziness. She understood them now — understood how fury and pain could drive a woman to do things that were totally out of character.

She was one of the lucky ones. The tranquility of her grandmother's house, distantly maintained by her and her siblings for those rare occasions when they were able to untangle their families from careers and life in general, had given her a haven. She had a place to go for shelter. A solid old structure, more stout than beautiful, weathered and enduring, Gran's house provided a refuge for squirrels in the woodpile, nectar for hungry hummingbirds in the array of whimsical feeders, and succor to a heartbroken woman. The structure cast its shadow far out over the flat, cold water her very own ancestors had christened Tear Lake — steady and unchanging except for the freeze and thaw cycle of nature.

Yet weeks later she was still unable to sleep. Leigh prowled the aged house in her worn flannel pajamas, listening to the familiar creak of the wooden floorboards beneath her bare feet. Night after night it had been the same. But tonight there was a new sound, a dull thud from the attic overhead.

"Squirrels," she told herself, shocked at how flat and dry her voice sounded. She hadn't spoken to anyone in days. She refused to answer the phone, ignoring the blinking red light as message after message was disregarded. She started to ignore the muffled sound above, but on the off chance it wasn't squirrels, that the sound might be a harbinger of something damaging to the old house she loved, she roused herself. With a weary sigh she climbed the narrow stairs to the attic, her bare toes curling over the edge of the thin treads. It was her responsibility to see the house maintained while she was here, and Leigh had always taken care of her responsibilities.

She flipped the switch and a bare bulb flickered to life. It cast a ring of stark light in the very center of the attic but left the corners in deep shadow. The whomp of wood striking on wood and the faint squeak of an ancient hinge brought her spinning around. The wind had blown open the octagonal window that sat in the apex of the eaves. With each gust it swung back on the hinges to hammer against the side of the house. Leigh leaned out and grabbed it, latched it in place but in the process she stubbed her little toe on a trunk.

"Ouch!" She grabbed her toes, sucking air

through her teeth as she hopped on one foot. She squinted at her throbbing digit in the harsh light.

"No blood. I'll live." Gingerly, doing an awkward heel walk, she stepped around the trunk to grab one of the leather handles and pull it out of the way.

"Ugh." Her shoulder hurt from the effort and she hadn't budged it an inch. Swathed in gossamer cobwebs, gilded in a layer of fine dust, it was too heavy to move by herself. Not so long ago it would've been second nature to ask Phillip, the rat, to help her. Now she would have to cope with this little domestic crisis alone. Alone, because her foolish husband had placed so little value on her love. The thought strengthened her resolve to be strong and self-reliant.

"Maybe I can unload a bit of the junk and move it." Her voice didn't have the reassuring sound she had hoped for. She lifted the lid and peered inside.

The smell of ancient wool tickled her nose as a shaft of flickering light from the solitary bulb fell over the contents. She picked up a handful of clothing and set it on the floor. Then her hand bumped against something hard and slender. She picked it up and discovered she was holding a small journal; the yellowed pages fell open about three-quarters of the way through.

*20 January, 1850. We buried twenty men today.*

The ink had faded a bit and Leigh had to squint to read the next line.

*What will happen now, I dare not guess. Will the wound of Tear Lake's heart ever heal?*

A question written long ago, but it tugged at Leigh's mind and curiosity. Her own soul had been bruised and deeply wounded by her husband's indiscretion. At this moment she wondered if she could ever heal. She longed for peace and some semblance of closure, but to do that she needed to have a firm idea of what she wanted. Right now she didn't have a clue. Phillip had betrayed her trust and she was angry — very angry. And the unfaithful rat was on her mind morning, noon and night, yet she didn't know what she wanted — what she needed — to do in order to exorcise the demon of his memory.

One hot tear landed on the cover of the slender book in her hand. The moisture dampened the powdery dust and revealed part of a gold filigree curl on the fine, tooled leather cover. Leigh rubbed her hand over the surface and found three letters.

*CRT*

An ancestor? Man? Woman? Leigh didn't

know. The script was flowery and small. The author was probably some past relation, since the trunk had obviously resided in Gran's attic for many years.

Leigh had never been interested in her family tree. That was her sister Vivian's department — Vivian, who had understood Leigh's need for time alone when she called and told her that she was going to Tear Lake.

"Go to Gran's house. Come to terms and then decide what you want to do. Divorce him. Teach him a lesson. Make him pay for what he did. But do what you need to do for you. Phil is an idiot. I expected better of him."

"So did I, Viv," Leigh said aloud. But then her sister had never given her heart to a man; she had remained single and alone because she couldn't risk the pain. Had she been right all along? Was it better to deny oneself a little happiness so there was no risk of disappointment and hurt?

She took a deep breath and promised herself that she wouldn't think of Phil for at least twenty minutes. He didn't deserve to take up so much of her day. She forced her mind back to the book. Had one of her predecessors owned it? Someone of her blood who had once walked beside the lake and watched the same sunsets and perhaps had endured a broken heart?

That thought gave her a strange sense of belonging. She had been so adrift since that late night phone call shattered her personal illusion of happily-ever-after. This old book was like a lifeline, a link between her and someone from the ancient times of this old house's history. It made her feel less alone, as if the person who wrote it was reaching out from the past to share secret confidences that would help Leigh find a way out of being stuck. Whatever the story within, it was a long one — was it happy? Full of encouragement? Did the person who wrote it find happily-ever-after?

Leigh flipped to a page near the beginning of the volume. The words there made her chest ache with longing and regret.

*Spring has come at last. And soon I'll celebrate my seventeenth birthday. I'm a woman fully grown and I'm ready to give my heart to someone. Please, Lord, hurry, I pray. Send him to me so I may begin my life.*

"So it was a young woman who wrote this, young and full of hope and confidence for a happy life."

Leigh wanted to know how the story ended. For the first time since arriving at the lake, she had a spark of curiosity and interest in something outside herself. If she nurtured that ember, maybe it would ignite a fire to burn away the dull apathy that made her feel old and tired and used up when she was barely middle-aged.

Copper wind chimes hanging from the eaves of the house pealed a haunting waltz composed by the night breezes that caressed the high mountains of Colorado as she walked down the stairs from the attic. She would fix a cup of tea and settle down to read the old journal — that would occupy her mind.

Leigh went to her room and changed into a comfortable old sweatshirt and pants and pulled on soft scrunchy socks. She padded into the front parlor, decorated in unintentional shabby chic, each piece a favored bit of furniture left by some former mistress of the house. She put the book on the barley leg table beside Gran's overstuffed chintz chair. The arms, covered in soft, worn, fabric and crocheted doilies, had offered an odd sort of comfort to Leigh. Now they beckoned her to sit and read. There had been a time when safety, love and reassurance had lived in her husband's embrace.

How could such love simply be gone? If it was a real love, could it simply cease to exist overnight?

*But it wasn't overnight. You have to admit that now,* the hard inner voice said with a bitterness that shook Leigh. She didn't want to turn into a sour, unforgiving woman forever marked by this event, but she had no idea how to take the high road and go on with the rest of her life.

She was stuck. And the place she was stuck in wasn't a pleasant place to be. She shivered with that thought and the chill in the room. The fire in the stone hearth had burned down but flared to life, embers curling into ebony whorls, the instant she added a few short lengths of well-seasoned aspen wood. She moved from the warmth of the fire into the kitchen. But that room held the gloom that comes from a house being nearly empty: every sound, every movement seemed loud and lonely. Leigh ignored those negative feelings and filled the old speckled kettle. Sulfur stung her nose when she struck a match to light the ancient gas cooker, the flame being born on a soft whomp of sound.

The chimes clanged while the back screen door rattled in its frame as the mountain winds gained strength. This time of year the weather was unsettled and volatile, much like her own soul. Leigh looked out the kitchen window over the sink to see the first salmon glow of dawn. There was a moment when the sun hung suspended, as if time had halted in the Rockies, then, in a stunning display, fingers of light spilled over the rim of the mountain and down into the valley. Red streaks shot across the rippled surface of the lake. It was glorious and she marveled that she still could appreciate such beauty.

"Guess I'm not completely dead inside."

As quickly as the sun rose, storm clouds began to scud across the sky, whipping whitecaps across the lake. A few small rowboats bobbed near the shore and the rickety old pier that had been there as long as she could remember. Lightning flashed in the eastern sky followed by a rumble of thunder rolling through the valley. The storm broke suddenly, sending torrents of rain pelting against the windows of the old house.

The scream of the teakettle startled Leigh. She spun around, her heart pounding. Her hands were shaking when she shut off the flame and moved the old graniteware pot to an iron trivet. Suddenly the old house seemed so — desolate.

So much of her identity had been wrapped up in being Phillip's wife. It wasn't that she didn't have interests and skills of her own, but she had always catered to Phillip. Her days revolved around him and she had done her best to be a good wife.

"The jerk. I gave him the best years of my life." The words sounded like a bad Hollywood script. "Jilted wife runs mad and starts talking to herself. I need a pet." She laughed but it sounded a little too high-pitched and a whole lot desperate. Was she becoming hysterical?

It wouldn't come as a big surprise. She had nearly made herself ill trying to understand what Phil had done. Was she not pretty enough? — or exciting enough? — or young enough? Was youth more important to him than devotion, fidelity, and years of history?

Though Phil had committed the sin, she had allowed it — accepting the thinnest of excuses when he returned home late, turning a blind eye to the emotional distance that had risen like a brick wall between them. His aversion to carrying a cell phone — now she saw that for what it truly had been.

"He didn't want me to be able to reach him."

His annoyance when she inquired about his day. To his guilty mind it had felt like an interrogation instead of the interest she had in his life.

Leigh sighed and rolled her shoulders, trying to shrug off the weight of failure. At least Cassie was settled in London, living the life of a single career girl. How much worse it would be if she were home to witness the shattering of her parents' twenty-year marriage. Leigh had managed to sound normal when she called and told Cass she was staying in Tear Lake for a while.

And Phillip . . . well, she didn't know where Phil was at the moment. Probably didn't want to know, but she could just imagine where he was — with his *thirty-something Twinkie,* a woman who had torn apart two marriages, her own and Leigh's.

"And why? Phillip is a fine-looking man, but he's almost fifteen years older — or is it his age and stability that makes him irresistible? I suppose being youthful enough to land a younger girlfriend has bolstered his ego. Yea, but what will he be like in ten years? I hope his hairline recedes and he gets a belly."

As if her bitter wish had unleashed some primal power that could bring about dire consequences, an explosion rocked the house. Leigh instinctively turned away from the window and covered her face with her hands. Shards of glass pelted her back as the window blew inward. Needles of hot pain sizzled along her bare forearms. The scent of burning wood filled the air. Energy crackled and snapped all around her. She couldn't help but turn her head and look through the shattered window. A torch of flame now blazed where a towering sugar pine had stood only moments ago. Scarred, blackened and gouged, the bark was split wide open. Resin-rich wood crackled as the flames shot upward, consuming the tree like a hungry monster.

"Lightning. It was lightning," she said in awe as her mind processed the devastation. Bits of wood and green needles lay on the old linoleum floor among the shards of broken glass. For a moment Leigh could only stand and gape at the destruction. Pinpoints of pain marked each spot of embedded glass on her bloody arms.

"Phil will have to replace the window —" she murmured before she caught herself. No, not Phillip, never Phil again.

"*Someone* will have to replace the window," she corrected sternly, chiding her foolish heart for not remembering. There was nobody but her to cope with this crisis. Suddenly she was galvanized to action. She grabbed the phone and jabbed 911.

"Yes, there has been a lightning strike just

above the lake on old Bend Road. Right, uh-huh. Thank you."

Tear Lake was a small town. News had traveled fast. The fire department was already on the way. Leigh yanked the phone book out of the drawer and flipped it open. Scanning the Yellow Pages while she drew her finger down the column of print, she dialed the number of the first glazier she found listed. Mercifully he picked up on the third ring. She explained what had happened and he promised to come right out. When those tasks were accomplished she began to tremble.

It had always been that way with her. Cool in the crisis but, when the necessary things were done, she would begin to shiver and tremble. She was standing there in the kitchen, surrounded by shards of shattered glass, shaking like an aspen in a strong Colorado wind. She couldn't help but compare the ruins of the room to her own life.

Leigh didn't know how long she stood frozen and unthinking, but the scream of the fire trucks roused her. A few heartbeats later there was a knock on the back door. Leigh tiptoed carefully in her sock-feet. The door seemed far away and she felt as if she were moving in slow motion.

"Hello? I'm here to replace a broken window — ma'am?" The man opened the screen door and peered through the old-fashioned window of the kitchen door. She drew back the bolt on the lock and opened it.

"Of course, please come in. Watch out for the glass." She managed a shaky smile, but he wasn't looking at her. He was intent on surveying the damage, a low whistle eloquently summing up what he saw. Then he turned and gave her 100 percent of his attention, keen intelligence shining in his eyes.

"Are you cut? Are you hurt? You're white as a sheet." He frowned as he surveyed her from head to toe. Then his eyes narrowed and he looked at her in a different way, curious, inquiring.

"Leigh? Is it you?" He grinned in that awkward way a person does when trying to place a face from the past — a long-ago memory, foggy and not quite solid.

"Do I know you?" She scanned his even features, the brown eyes and warm concerned smile, but she couldn't dredge up any recognition on her part. This man was definitely a stranger to her.

"It is me, Brian Banyard. My uncle runs the local grocery. We used to argue over the deep fishing hole on the south side of the lake — the one by the old mine. You know, up Haunted Trail?"

Her brain took in all he said and suddenly she did know him — or the boy inside the man, at any rate. "Oh, yes, Brian. I'm sorry I didn't recognize you. Goodness, you have a good memory. That was a long time ago. I haven't been up here fishing since the summer I was sixteen and you were — what? — ten?"

"I was twelve that summer, thank you very much. Hey, Leigh, you're bleeding." He reached out and took hold of her elbow. "You need to sit down."

"No, I'm fine. I need to sweep up this glass." She swayed a little and her knees went rubbery. If not for the strong grip Brian had on her, she would surely have hit the floor among the broken glass. He guided her through the litter to a kitchen chair and against her will she sagged into it, stunned by her weakness.

"Are you here alone?" His voice turned a bit brittle and he looked beyond her into the other rooms.

"Yes, but I'm perfectly able to —"

"You're not going to do anything. I'm taking you into town. The urgent care center can treat those cuts. That branch didn't hit you or anything, did it?"

"Branch?" Sure enough, there was a large branch sticking through the window. He nudged the branch with the toe of his boot. Scorched pine needles were everywhere.

"I'm okay, really —"

"I don't know, Leigh, your eyes are awfully red." He gently tipped up her chin and looked deep into her eyes. Could he see her pain and humiliation? "There's not that much smoke in here. Are you seeing double or anything?"

"No, it's not that, I —" A million emotions flooded through her. It was on the tip of her tongue to admit she had been crying, that she had been dumped by her husband of twenty years and had come running up here to escape the humiliation, but she bit her tongue and just blinked at him.

"You poor kid, I think you're suffering from shock. Come on." He eased her out of the chair with a gentle pressure.

"But the window —"

"I'll fix it later."

"But the burning tree —"

"Is being taken care of. The burners are all off too so don't even ask about that. You're the most important thing, Leigh. Just let me take care of you."

*You're the most important thing, Leigh.* His words caused a sharp tug on her heart.

Hadn't Phillip once told her that? Funny how men all said the same thing at one time or another — did any of them ever really mean it?

Brian was guiding her to the front door when the phone rang. She lurched to a halt. "I — I should get that, it might be my sister."

"Stay right here, I'll take care of it. Whoever it is can call you back."

"But —"

"No buts, Leigh. You need medical attention, then when you have been given a clean bill of health you can return the call."

He grabbed the ringing phone. She heard his voice, brisk and efficient, "Sorry, Leigh has had a little accident. We're on our way to the emergency room. You will have to call her later. Sure, uh-huh. Bye." Within a moment he was back.

"Who was it?" She leaned into his strength.

"Somebody named Phillip."

# Two

Brian was a good driver. He had big capable hands that he kept fastened at ten and two, and he kept his attention on the road. He was making good time, a small blessing for which she was grateful. Her hands were still trembling and the glass shards that had ripped through the sweatshirt were beginning to hurt and burn even though there was little bleeding. She leaned back against the headrest.

"Ouch." She jerked away from the headrest.

"Are you okay?" Brian flicked a concerned glance her way.

"I must have broken glass embedded in the back of my scalp." She leaned awkwardly toward the dash, feeling a little queasy as Brian accelerated a bit more. The trees blurred in her peripheral vision.

"The emergency room folks will get you fixed up. You know I heard you got married and moved to Pine Crest. I guess living in a city that large is like going to the far side of the moon after little ol' Tear Lake."

"Small town living has some advantages that I haven't really appreciated until recently," Leigh murmured, realizing that Brian was trying to engage her in conversation and keep her mind off her injuries.

"I also heard your daughter went to England. Good for her."

"I'm surprised you know all that." And she was. It wasn't as if she was anyone special, so it startled her a bit that people in this small town would've kept up.

"That's the kind of thing that gets talked about a lot at church picnics and the like. You know how it is, small towns are a little like nosey family, we may not see each other regular, but we certainly know the skinny."

Leigh grimaced. She hoped that wasn't the case. One of the reasons she had come here was to escape the glances — the curious and the pitying.

He swung his pickup into the parking lot and under the covered ER entrance. Automatic doors swished open, beckoning her.

"Well, here we are, Leigh. You sit right there and I'll get a wheelchair."

"I can walk," she said, determined to stand on her own two feet. She lifted the door handle and shoved the door open. Brian was out and around the truck before she had moved.

"I know you can, but I want to push you in a wheelchair. I'll be the hero of the hour. You can't deny me my moment, now can you?" He chuckled and raised his pale blond brows, blocking the door with his solid body.

"If you put it that way, I guess not." She wasn't fooled for a minute by his argument, but she was grateful for his gallantry when he helped her from the cab of his pickup and her knees buckled. She was limp as a rag doll when he took her weight on his arm. For a moment she had a flash of concern. Were her injuries serious?

"Just hang in there, Leigh. Soon your pain will all be gone."

She silently wished he could make that happen. Was there anybody who could wash away the ache?

An hour later Leigh had been treated and given an injection of pain medication. She was blissfully numb from the drugs when Brian once again loaded her into his pickup with the strange wooden racks in the back. They held various sizes of glass panes, the sunlight creating prisms of light as they drove. A lovely song about being lifted up to stand on mountains was on the radio.

Brian hummed along to the melody as the truck swung back onto the road toward Gran's house. The green and brown blur of pine trees and the pretty blue of columbine flowers rushed by the window. Leigh rested her head against the cool glass on the passenger side and glanced at Brian from the corner of her eye. He had always been just a freckle-faced kid to her. Funny how she realized she had grown up, matured, aged, but expected other people to remain in some sort of time warp.

He was a good-looking guy, but more than that, he seemed to exude a kind of peace and quiet confidence — a sort of instinctive attitude of assurance, as if he was certain that everything would be all right. If only she could find something in her life to make her feel that way. If only there was an inoculation against the doubt and disillusionment of life.

As they made the last turn and her grandmother's house came into view, it was as if all the pain medication simply evaporated. Her scalp burned, her arms stung and ached beneath the bandages. The raw wound in her heart opened anew. She was barely able to drag air into her lungs, the emotional bereavement was such a physical force.

"Hey, you have a visitor. Do you feel up

to seeing anybody?" Brian asked as he parked the pickup and turned off the engine. "Nice-looking fella, tall, dark and a bit edgy, I think you ladies say."

"No, I don't want to talk to him." Leigh was a coward; she knew it and hated that weakness had crippled her, but she wasn't ready to see Phillip. She was afraid of what she might do or say. She couldn't bear the thought of losing control and acting like a demented woman in front of Brian — not after he had been so nice. Then again . . . was she in any shape to whack Phillip upside the head? Probably not, since she was rubbery kneed from the pain meds. Maybe she should talk to him. He was relatively safe from any homicidal urges she might have while she was on drugs. She could barely see straight, so she couldn't very well hit him. But then again, how much energy and strength would it take to shove him into all the glass in the back of Brian's truck? She shook herself, banishing the thoughts of violence and revenge.

"Perhaps you could just help me inside?" Leigh asked Brian.

"Sure. Who is he, Leigh?"

"Phillip. My soon-to-be ex-husband."

Brian's smile slipped and his face reddened a bit. Then his embarrassment faded away and an expression of such compassion, such empathy, filled his eyes that Leigh wanted to crawl into a hole somewhere. Why was it that Phil's betrayal had become her shame? Why did she feel dirty and degraded because he had been unfaithful?

"Leigh, please —" Phillip reached out as if to touch her as Brian hustled her up the steps. They had to stop to unlock the door — it took too long. Phillip had followed them up the steps to the long wraparound porch. Now his hand was there, reaching out to her, but she stared mutely at it until he let it fall limply to his side.

"Are you okay? What happened?" He sounded tired — weary. A part of her gladdened to see he wasn't happy-go-lucky while the habits of twenty years of marriage made her want to give him some comfort.

Silly woman.

"I won't talk to you. Haven't you noticed I've been letting the machine pick up your messages. You really should leave now, Phillip, or I'm not going to be responsible for what I might do to you — you jerk." Then she halted and stared at him, rage, pain and her medication blending like a cocktail in her veins. "Why are you here? Isn't it bad enough you have broken my heart? And now you have to show up here — here, where I'm struggling to find peace and become a sane, reasonable woman again? I can't cope with it — not now — not here. Go away." She swayed a bit on her feet and had to grip the doorjamb to steady herself.

Brian's jaw dropped and Phil's eyes grew round. She scuttled into the house before the first dry sob broke. She shut the door and turned the deadbolt, leaning against it while the crushing pain washed over her in a great, cold wave. It took her several minutes to blink the blur from her eyes. Then she staggered to the old sofa and collapsed, closing her eyes against the light and the dull scratchy pain from crying. The scent of pine smoke lingered in the air. She realized that the kitchen window was still shattered, the floor littered with glass. She couldn't deal with it — not now. Maybe later, but not now.

The back door opened and closed.

If Phil had come in without being invited, she would hit him with Gran's favorite cast-iron skillet. What had he done to her? She was becoming a violent person full of rage, seeking revenge. That wasn't the person she was inside and definitely not the person she wanted to show to the world, yet the demons of retribution urged her on.

"Phillip — I swear I'll not be —" She

levered herself up on the sofa, summoning the last of her strength, preparing to do battle when Brian's ever-cheerful face appeared in the doorway.

"It's just me, Leigh. I'm going to replace the window and clean up this glass. You rest now, and I'll lock up when I finish. I'm leaving my card by the phone, if you need anything, you just call."

"Brian, I don't know how to thank you —"

"You know what Luke says."

"Luke?" she asked numbly. "Luke who?" Had she missed part of the conversation? The last time she looked it was only Brian and Phil, the unfaithful rat. When did Luke show up?

"The book of Luke — in the Good Book. 'Do unto others, as you would have them do unto you.' Or there is Phillippians 2:4 . . . 'Each of you should look out for the interests of others.' No need for thanks — you're Tear Lake family, Leigh."

Oh great. First Phillip shows up to make her crazy and now Brian is spouting scripture at her. What's up with that? Is he one of those Bible-thumping weirdoes? Is he going to start knocking on her door every other day to try and get her into church? If he turned out to be a Jesus-freak stalker, she wasn't sure she could cope with that either. All this rushed through her drugged brain and she didn't know what to say, but he saved her the trouble of trying to think of the right words when he simply turned and went back into the kitchen.

Leigh flopped back on the sofa, closed her eyes and wondered what other calamities would befall her today as she drifted off into a painkiller-induced sleep.

The phone woke Leigh from a deep, dreamless sleep. She lurched to her feet, feeling thick-tongued and cotton-headed. She stumbled into the kitchen and picked up the ringing phone.

"Leigh?" It was Phillip's voice. "For pity sake, Leigh, what happened? That guy wouldn't tell me anything."

"I'm on drugs so this is obviously a product of my imagination — a delusion. Because why — I ask you why — would the man who cheated on me for a younger woman, the man who wanted out of our marriage because he wanted to find a new life, be calling me? I can't think of a single solitary reason, so I'm hanging up now. Good-bye, delusion." Leigh slammed down the phone. She was stunned by the bitterness in her sarcastic words. She was becoming someone she didn't like.

There were a hundred things she should have said to him. Like, "I've cried more in the last few weeks than I did in our twenty years of marriage," or "I thought I knew you, Phil. I put all my trust in you — you no-good, lying, cheating rat."

Then her gaze fell on the card by the phone. The print was plain and dark.

*Brian Banyard, Glazier. You break it; I'll make it whole.* She picked it up and turned it over. There was another line written in a neat hand.

*If you will let him, God will make you whole and heal your wounds easier than I can replace a broken pane of glass. He can give you a miracle if you will only ask.*

"I'm not sure I believe in miracles anymore," Leigh said aloud as she used a push-pin to skewer the business card to the corkboard beside the phone.

Sleeping in her bed was impossible. The places where the emergency room doctor removed the glass were not deep, but each one was very uncomfortable. She was a patchwork quilt of Band-Aids, two-by-two squares of white gauze and surgical tape. Finally at two o'clock in the morning she gave up trying to find a position where her head and arms didn't pinch when she dozed off, and retreated from the bedroom. Wearing her baggiest, softest sweats, with one of Gran's colorful memory quilts tucked under her arm, she went downstairs. In moments she had a fire going in the hearth and a cup of hot cocoa on the table beside the overstuffed chair. She picked up the small red journal she had found in the attic.

Leigh opened the book at the first page and ran her finger across the neat writing. She settled down to read each line and was swept back in time to those early days. Through the young girl's eyes she saw a ramshackle community of tents and small cabins. Tear Lake had been founded as a silver and gold mining camp back in the mid-1800s. The town was a wonderful mix of residents who could trace their roots to Wales, Bohemia, Germany, Cornwall and Ireland. Rich traditions from all those lands were deeply woven into the texture of life in the tiny community.

Contemporary travel guides compared Tear Lake to an Alpine village. Skiing — both water and snow — boating, hiking, hunting, fishing and just plain soaking up the beauty of nature were the activities that brought tourists to Tear Lake, but when the author of the journal arrived, only one rutted road led in and out of town. However, a thousand tiny trails meandered into the high canyons, valleys and ravines that scarred the mountain where miners coaxed gold and silver from the rock. Leigh was able to visualize the majestic valley and pristine wilderness. She grew anxious to know more and impulsively flipped ahead in the journal.

There was a terrible accident at one of the mines today. The smell and taste of dust, the screaming of the small ponies, the horrible thunder of the cave-in, is something I shall never be able to banish from my memory.

Leigh pulled the old quilt up to her chin while images of such a horrible calamity chilled her. She continued to read out of sequence.

Papa and some of the other men dug with shovels late into the night. The flickering of their lanterns winking in the darkness made me think of angels sent by the Lord. When dawn came they began to pull the dead men from the mine shaft. Their wives, daughters and sons stood by, white-faced, keening their sorrow. I was proud of Papa. He stood tall, though his skin was gray from fatigue and the dust of digging. He quoted from the Bible, and his words are now burned into my heart. "Bow down thine ear to me; deliver me speedily: be thou my strong rock, for an house of defense to save me. For thou art my rock and my fortress; therefore for thy name's sake lead me, and guide me." I'm so consumed with sadness but I'm also comforted by those words.

Leigh let the journal rest in her lap while she sipped her cocoa. She thought about all the loves and sorrows that had played out in the little town. Her current heartbreak was just one of many. But how did those people go on? Were they stronger back then? Or were they like Brian, who had faith in God and therefore didn't feel pain in the same way she did? The lack of God in her life was becoming a constant question, waiting there at the edge of her mind, popping up at the most unexpected times. She almost felt as if some inner voice were talking to her, coaxing her — but to what destination she didn't know.

The intrusion of the phone ringing brought a frown to her face. Leigh hated it when the phone rang at night — it usually heralded bad news.

"Hello?"

"Hey, Li-Li."

Her eldest brother's gravelly voice rolled over her. She glanced at the clock on the mantel. "Tom, what are you doing up so early?"

"Time zone, sis, time zone. Did I wake you?"

"No, I haven't been sleeping a lot."

"Been there. What can I do to help?" Tom's wife of twenty-five years had divorced him last year. The entire family had been shocked. Rosemary had simply packed a bag and walked out of everyone's life. Leigh had never asked Tom about the reason — she had been too embarrassed and unwilling to intrude on his privacy. Now the question hung, unspoken. Finally she dredged up the courage and asked, "Tom, what happened between you and Rosie?"

The silence on the other end of the line was deafening. For a moment she thought he might have hung up and she chided herself for having been so stupid as to ask. Then she heard Tom heave a sigh.

"I've asked myself that same question and I think I finally came up with an answer. I was a lousy husband."

"No, Tom —"

"It is true, Li-Li. I was a good provider

but I wasn't there — you know what I mean? I was selfish with my time. Rosie should have left me long before she did. At first I thought maybe if we had kids, but that wasn't the problem. She tried to . . . engage me, I guess you could say, more than once through the years, but I just wouldn't do it. If I had it all to do over, believe me, I'd be a different kind of man. But after the divorce Rosie just sort of blossomed, and I realized how I had held her back — or at least didn't do anything to encourage her growth. She sure doesn't need me now. I still love her but . . ."

"I'm sorry, Tom. I shouldn't have asked."

"No, I'm glad you did. What're you going to do, Leigh? Do you need any help — financial help?"

"No. I'm fine for a while at least."

"And how are you holding up? I mean emotionally? Is it a good idea to stay at Gran's house all alone?"

"I decided being alone was the best course of action when I found myself standing in Phillip's side of the closet with a pair of shears in one hand and his favorite sports coat in the other."

"Ouch."

Leigh laughed mirthlessly. "Better his suits than him. But all joking aside, I realized I was letting anger control me. I was losing my mind and becoming some sort of borderline-homicidal harpy."

"Maybe you were entitled," Tom said dryly. "I could come have a little . . . uh . . . talk with Phillip."

"Thanks, but that wouldn't accomplish anything. I can't force him to love me and want to be faithful."

"Have you talked to an attorney?"

Well, there it was: the question that put it all in perspective.

"Not yet."

"Leigh — you do want a divorce don't you?"

"He cheated on me, Tom. I mean, what choice but divorce is there? I'm not going to be a doormat. I'm not going to be one of those women who turns a blind eye while her husband skips blithely from one affair to the next. It is me all the way, or no way. I deserve at least that. Phillip knew how I felt about spouses who cheat and it didn't hold him back."

"Yeah, I get what you're saying. But do you still love him?"

Did she?

"If I did, wouldn't I be kind of pathetic? I mean, what kind of masochist loves somebody who rips her heart out?"

Tom sighed again. "You tell me and we'll both know. Just sleep on it, kid. Take some time, don't do anything rash you may regret. A house is just a big empty house when you live alone."

"I could buy a dog."

"I bought two, but it is still not a home without Rosie."

"Tom, why don't you come visit me? We could rattle around here in Gran's house together. I found this great old journal in the attic. Which reminds me, do you know if we had any relatives with the last initial of T?"

"T? No, none that I can recall. Nana was an Abbott before she married, and her mother was Reynolds. You should ask Viv."

"I'll do that. And Tom, I mean it. Come stay here at Tear Lake for a while."

"You can't run from yourself, kid. Remember that."

"I love you, Tom."

"I love you, too. Bye."

Leigh hung up the phone and stood there staring at the blinking light on the answering machine. Eventually she would have to talk to Phil.

And then it hit her. Phillip was here — in Tear Lake, not back in the city. There was only one logical reason he had tracked her down. He had come here to ask her for a divorce. Suddenly all the air and warmth went out of the room.

"Phillip wants to hurry and get divorced so he will be free to marry his Twinkie."

Dawn was breaking over the rim of the mountain, all pink, purple and new. The weather was lovely; a soft mountain breeze was moving the tops of the tall pine trees in a gently swaying motion. Lower down the mountain the aspens shuddered, light winking off the leaves while a soft sigh of sound descended. Her conversation with Tom kept playing over and over in her head. The sheltering walls of Gran's house seemed to be closing in on her. She had done nothing but think in circles since she arrived here.

"I've got to get some fresh air." The desperation in her own voice caught her unaware.

Leigh put on a thick sweater, jeans and a light jacket. Then she made herself a thermos of hot cocoa and set a course toward the mountain. She walked the well-trod path around the lake, reveling in the feel of the early morning sun on her face, the breeze in her hair and the solitude. It brushed along her shoulders like the caress of butterfly wings. In the distance she saw something winking bright and metallic in the sunshine. She wasn't sure what it was, but she used it as a beacon, taking long, purposeful strides toward it.

The sun broke full over the mountain and showered golden, warm rays down into the valley. The nearer she came, the brighter the reflected object became. She rounded a bend in the path, flanked by tall pines, and found herself staring at the backside of the little whitewashed church. The glistening object was now hidden or the sun had passed its zenith, because she couldn't see it. She stepped from behind the church and was engulfed in a great crowd of people.

The summers she had spent with Nana had been idyllic days of exploration, but she'd never been inside the church. Her family was composed of good people, salt-of-the-earth folk, but none of them had been churchgoers. As a child she remembered feeling a certain hollowness when her friends attended this church, the Sunday service a ritual and part of their lives. As she grew older she had intended to go, but there was always something — the urge to sleep in — a backyard barbeque — lazy days spent with Phillip and her daughter.

She blinked away the memory and focused on her surroundings. There was a cemetery at the far side of the church, and several gaily dressed women were putting fresh flowers on graves scattered throughout the pine-shaded graveyard. Giggling little girls, dressed in the hues of those same spring flowers, scampered around metal chairs that had been set up in neat rows. Men in suits gathered in small clutches, holding Bibles, speaking in low tones. One of the men raised his head and waved at Leigh.

It took her a moment to realize it was Brian Banyard. She almost didn't recognize him in a suit and tie, his thatch of unruly hair tamed by gel. He cleaned up real nice.

"Leigh. How wonderful to see you here."

"It's so early, what is going on?"

He laughed and took her hand. "Today is Easter, Leigh. We're here for sunrise service, and evidently God has led you here to listen to the message as well. Let me introduce you to some of your neighbors before the service begins."

"But I'm not dressed —" She looked down at her jeans and sneakers.

"God cares about the garments of your soul, Leigh, not the clothes you wear to hear His word."

In spite of Brian's insistence that Leigh sit up front, she found a chair in the last row.

Pastor Miller, who had a full head of snowy white hair and rosy cheeks, possessed a mellow, deep voice that needed no microphone to be heard. He read passages from the Bible, and unlike the uneasy feeling she had when Brian quoted scripture to her the other day, the words seemed different. They touched her heart, and made her question not only her own existence, but once again she wondered if a God-based belief system was the key to happiness. It wasn't that she didn't believe in God; she did. But her relationship with Him was casual, to say the least. She listened intently and realized that she had never been saved, never been baptized. She didn't understand the whole born-again thing. It was something she just hadn't given much thought to — until now. She was still pondering when a few people drifted toward the pastor at the front of the gathering. She was watching them beneath her lashes when she recognized one of the men. The morning sun turned his hair to a dark, burnished ash. He looked thinner; lines of determination etched his lean face.

It was Phil. She had to consciously keep herself in the uncomfortable chair while she struggled with the impulse to run to the sanctuary of Gran's house. A streak of stubborn pride was all that held her rooted to the spot.

"You can't run from yourself," Tom had said. And she couldn't run from Phillip either. It was time to start acting like an adult. Her broken heart was still raw and aching, but she couldn't pull the covers over her head and hide any longer.

She watched him from the corner of her eyes, trying not to look directly at him while a hundred primal emotions ran through her. He spoke with several men, then Pastor Miller.

What was he saying now with his head bent, standing beside the pastor? And where was his Twinkie girlfriend? Leigh barely resisted the impulse to scan the crowd. What would she do if she saw her? She hadn't come face-to-face with her — was she tough enough to endure it? Or would she scream and throw a tantrum and shame herself?

Then mercifully the service was over. People were drifting away. If she hurried she could spare herself the misery of encountering the woman. Leigh scooped up her thermos of untouched chocolate and set off briskly toward Gran's house. She wasn't going to continue being a victim, but she wasn't going to stand around and invite disaster either. It was time to pluck up her courage, dust off her knees and get on with life. If Phil was here to discuss divorce, then let him. She would find a way to cope with the pain and rejection, but she wasn't going to do it with an audience.

That night she waited for the phone to ring while she snuggled down with the little journal again, but this time she drank strong sweet tea and opened the book to the front and started at the very beginning. It was time to show a little discipline in all areas of her life. No more skipping to the backs of the books to read the endings.

She was going to discover the story from the first word to the last.

*March 2, 1859*

We arrived today. The journey has been long, first by boat, then wagon and finally the last by foot. Mama has left behind nearly everything, including Granny's reed organ and her small spinning wheel. She was so overset that she fell to her knees beside the lake and wept that the journey was over. By nightfall the miners had begun calling it Tear Lake, named for my mama's tears. Papa promises all will be well. I believe him when he says our lives will be different — better somehow. But inside I'm afraid.

*March 15, 1859*

I'm so angry. Today another group of immigrants arrived. Papa says they are from Bohemia. Some of the other men in town shun them and made them pitch their small camp far away from the others. We are all new here. How can anybody think they have more right? Papa says little but I know he is going to do something.

*March 17, 1859*

I knew Papa would do something. I am so proud. He has started building a church. It is going to be beautiful and he has told all the miners that everyone will be welcome. Even though he is not a minister, he has been responsible for prayer meetings and now he is doing what is right. I know it is not right to be prideful, but I am so happy he is my papa!

# THREE

The ringing phone woke Leigh. The suddenness made her heart beat fast and she was a bit disoriented. Then it all came flooding back — where she was and why. She hesitated to answer, but only for a moment. Then she decided dealing with phone calls was probably a good first step in behaving like an adult and moving forward with her life. She was tired of feeling like a victim. It was time to demonstrate she had a backbone like her pioneer ancestors.

"Hello." She half-expected to hear Phillip's voice. Instead it was soft, feminine and brought a lump to her throat.

"Mom?" There was love and concern in that one word. A lifetime of memories of scraped knees, freckles, tears and humility. She had avoided calling Cassie for a couple of weeks because she didn't know what to say — hadn't really wanted to speak poorly of Phil so she had simply told her daughter she was spending a while at Gran's house.

"Are you all right? I just heard . . . what happened? Do I need to come home?"

"No."

"No, you aren't all right, or no, I don't need to fly home?"

The tears that thickened Cassie's words made Leigh angry with Phil all over again. How could he have done this? How could he hurt his only child with some silly mid-life crisis?

"You do not need to come home. I'm . . . getting by."

"Oh, Mom, I don't know what to say. I mean, Daddy . . . I'd never have thought. I'm so sorry."

"Wait, don't say another word. You haven't anything to feel sorry about. Your father made this mess, not you. I refuse to feel guilty and I don't want you to, either."

Leigh sounded so convincing. But it would serve no purpose for Cassie to know that each night in the dark, when sleep would not come, Leigh went over every deed, every mistake she had made in her marriage. She might say she wasn't sharing Phil's guilt, but she was, as surely as if she had been the one casting an eye about for a younger partner — of course that thought was ludicrous. She wanted a man to stand shoulder to shoulder with her, not someone who had a mother fixation. "Tadpoling" was the term Hollywood had given to the young men who escorted older women. "Cougar" was the term for the aging female — not a very complimentary term and one Leigh never wanted attached to her name. Tadpole or Twinkie, the idea was simply laughable. Leigh just didn't understand this sudden craze for marrying someone young enough to be one's child. Whatever happened to forever? What about commitment and maturity and growing old together? Who in their right mind wanted to try and keep up, or to feel like they were raising someone?

"Mom, are you there?" Cassie's voice yanked Leigh back to the present.

"Cassie, I know this will be hard for you, but you have to go on as before. Phillip has always been a good father. I don't expect, or want, you to take sides in this."

"It's so hard, Mom."

"I know."

"I mean, of course I love Daddy, but I'm so disappointed in him. It is like I never knew him — you know? The fact that he could — I just never believed my daddy would do something like this."

"Yes, I understand. But I want you to put it out of your mind, as much as you can.

Go on with your life. Your father and I've got to find a way to do the same. Uncle Tom called and we talked. I think it is time to call an attorney."

"Mom? Is this really what you want? I mean, could you ever forgive him?"

Leigh took a deep breath. The very question she had been asking herself. Was she ready to speak to a lawyer or was there even the ghost of a chance — but what was she saying? Phillip had brought another woman into their sphere.

"I don't know, Cassie. I honestly don't know. What other option is there except divorce? Phillip is . . . involved. Right now I can't see anything changing. Your father wants out. I don't want to be one of those women who fights for a faded love. Either he loves me or he doesn't. And as much as I don't want to speak ill of your father, his actions have been eloquent on the subject of where his heart lies. And Cassie?"

"Yes?"

"Who told you?"

"Daddy. He called me last night. He said he wanted me to hear from him how sorry he was."

Leigh thought about that. At least Phillip was sorry about upsetting Cassie. That was something; it just wasn't nearly enough.

■ ■ ■ ■

An hour later Leigh sat at the table on the outside patio with a cup of hot tea and the little journal in her hand. The book fell open much farther than she had read last night. Even though she had made the decision to start reading from the beginning, she couldn't resist; she had no willpower. Her eyes skimmed over the first line.

*Can I ever forgive him?*

The words leaped off the page. It was as if a voice from the past was trying to tell her something. Leigh continued to read. *If he has done what everyone thinks, can I forgive him? He made promises to me. Will I ever be able to say the name of—*

Leigh turned the page but the next line made no sense. She flipped back to the previous page. The last entry had ended abruptly just before a name had been written.

She frowned at the book and held it nearer. When she bent the spine and forced it wide, she could just see where a page had been torn away.

"How odd." She thumbed through the journal and found several other places where pages were missing. And at the very back she found a flower, yellowed with age, and pressed flat. It wasn't a variety she recognized. There were many wildflowers that grew in abundance in the lee side of the mountain each spring when the snow melted and life burst from the earth. But she had never seen one like this. It was once undoubtedly snowy white, with a touch of pink at the tip of each sharp petal. A bit of rough, spiky leaf was still attached to the stem.

"How peculiar. A unique flower and missing pages — an old mystery has been waiting in Gran's trunk." The journal had been packed away in the attic for years and years. But someone had removed pages from the little book long ago. She couldn't help but wonder why.

"And those pages contained the name of a person who had evidently abandoned the author, and was suspected of taking some sort of treasure," Leigh murmured. So much for a happily-ever-after ending to the tale. She sipped her tea and turned back to the front of the volume. There was only one way to find out what had happened, and that was to read it all as it had been recorded. She set the cup down and picked up where she had left off, reading about the raw frontier of the mining community.

*June 27, 1859*

I'm crying as I write this. Today was supposed to be the most joyous new beginning. We have all our barrels packed and loaded into the skid. But we will not move into our new house today. There was a terrible accident at one of the mines. The smell and taste of dust, the screaming of the small ponies, the horrible thunder of the cave-in is something I shall never forget. I find comfort in my Bible. Papa says God has a great plan but in times like this I lack the strength of my faith because I find myself questioning and wondering why this has happened.

The phone rang. Leigh didn't budge, but it wasn't because she was hiding; it was because she was too comfortable, or at least that was the lie she told herself. After six rings she heard the machine pick up.

"Leigh? Leigh? I know you're there. It is Phillip. Pick up the phone. Please."

Leigh sighed and set the book aside. For all her determination to face her problems, she couldn't talk to him. And yet she couldn't enjoy the book if he continued to call. She thought of Tom and Cassie and her own confusion.

"Coward," she said aloud. But she just wasn't ready yet. She needed to be more in control before she opened herself up for the last stab of rejection from the man she had vowed to love forever.

So when the phone rang once again, she put the empty teacup in the sink and walked out the door. She could just hear Phil leaving another message as she stepped off the porch.

The day was glorious. A breeze moved the leaves and the tall grasses at the edge of the lane below Gran's house. Magpies, in dress black and white, flitted along the path that led to the church. The day beckoned — whispered to her — inviting her to meander down the road, to leave her problems behind. She found her feet moving of their own accord.

When she turned the bend and saw the church, a warm sensation of belonging washed through her, but she didn't understand how or why. She had only attended the one service; how could she feel so at home? Perhaps it was the kind eyes of Pastor Miller, or his rosy cheeks, making him look as if he had just come in from sledding down a snow-crusted slope of the mountain. Or perhaps it was simply the passages from the Bible that stuck in her mind and refused to be forgotten.

She was humming one of the songs sung by the choir when she saw a man in the cemetery. Silver shot through his dark hair, but he stood straight and tall. There was something almost familiar about him. She stopped to observe him.

"Leigh. What a pleasant surprise."

Leigh turned to find Brian Banyard behind her. His eyes were bright with interest and though it was rude, her first impulse was to turn away before he started quoting scripture to her. She had a warm, fuzzy feeling about the church, but she was still leery of him and how he could quote verses off the top of his head to fit a conversational situation. But before she could make up some excuse and scuttle away, he smiled and said, "I seem to keep bumping into you."

She glanced back at the man in the cemetery, hoping he might come over and join them, but he was moving away, almost lost in the long shadows of morning. He had left a spray of wild mountain flowers. Leigh cast around for something to say.

"It's nice to see someone honoring a loved one. I certainly don't put flowers on Gran's grave as often as I should. She and Grandpa are buried in the cemetery next to my great-grandparents."

"That is my grandfather who just left. He brings flowers regularly. He rode up with me today. I've a meeting here in a bit," Brian explained though she didn't ask. "My family has been here nearly as long as yours. A rock slide covered the back part of the cemetery a few years back, and we lost some of the older gravestones."

Leigh looked up the mountain. There was a scar of boulders where vegetation was only beginning to return. "I hadn't noticed before."

"One morning we heard a rumble and saw a slide. It was a small one, thank the Lord."

The sound of a motor hiccupping along the lane drew her attention to the narrow blacktopped road that flowed out from town. A bright yellow bus struggled around the bend and up the steep incline, forcing the driver to keep downshifting until the vehicle was almost at a standstill.

"Great, you're just in time to meet my kids," Brian said, turning from the cemetery and striding toward the front of the church. Now that he was leaving and Leigh had what she wanted, she decided she didn't want it. She trailed after him.

"Your kids? I — that is, I didn't know you were married."

"Engaged, but we haven't set a date. These are really God's children — as we all are. He only loans them to me for a few weeks each spring. Come and meet them."

Trying to ignore Brian's too-chipper Christian attitude but spurred on by her curiosity, Leigh walked to the edge of the road and watched as a dozen children emerged from the doors of the bus. Some were mentally challenged, some appeared to be bewildered and lost. Some just wore sadness like a tough coat of armor.

"Hi, kids. Glad to see you, I have been waiting." Then he turned toward Leigh and said, "For six weeks, these will be my children." Brian beamed at her. "They come from the inner city to spend a short while here in Tear Lake to enjoy God's beauty. Some of these kids have never been to church. We're going to remedy that. Others have never been allowed to run and play. Life can be tough for them, especially the ones stuck in a poor neighborhood. A lot of these kids come from single-parent households and they spend a lot of time either alone or with baby-sitters. If we had more money, we could make a greater impact, but the Lord will provide as He sees fit." He laughed as several of the children hugged his leg or grabbed hold of his hand. "My fiancée Shirley will be helping me in a few days, but she couldn't make it today since the lady she hired to take over the bakery for the summer was delayed by a family crisis."

It hit her then. Brian wasn't creepy or trying to be preachy when he spoke of God or quoted the Bible. He really believed every word he said — he was a genuinely nice guy. Feeling a little embarrassed for her past judgment about him, Leigh crouched down and smiled at one shy boy. He hesitated for only a moment, and then he propelled himself into her arms with such force she was nearly knocked flat.

"Hey, tiger. Who are you?" She smiled at the little boy who had obviously been born with Down's syndrome.

"This is Tim," Brian said. "Tim is a very special friend. His family used to live here in Tear Lake a while back. He comes every year. Don't you, Tim?"

Tim nodded his head and grinned.

"Then we're almost neighbors, aren't we, Tim?" Leigh smoothed his thatch of soft brown hair and smiled when he nodded in agreement.

"You're good with kids, Leigh." Brian sounded a little surprised, and she wondered if she should be annoyed.

"The love of a child is special — or at least I've always thought so." She smiled, remembering Cassie as a child, all giggling enthusiasm and curiosity.

"Listen, I don't know what your summer plans are, but if you have the time, maybe you'd like to volunteer to help out with the kids? At least until Shirley is free — a week or so at most."

"I don't know — I don't have any special qualifications."

"Hey, God gave you a loving heart. I think that is qualified enough. You raised a daughter — what more do you need?"

She thought about her schedule — then realized with a jolt she had no schedule. She didn't have to put a meal together — or go to the dry cleaners or shop for special foods or sit home by the phone in case Phil was running late. It hit her then that she had catered to Phillip. In fact, some time in the last twenty years, she had taken on the role of caretaker instead of partner. His life had been so well-ordered and organized by her efforts that he was able to focus exclusively on work and his own pleasure. She couldn't remember the last time he'd had to cancel a golf game or bowling date with the guys in order to do something for her. If the furnace needed repair or the car required service, she took care of it. If the lawn service couldn't come, she pushed the mower around the yard. She had a stepladder to take care of the lightbulbs and had taken a class at the junior college so she was able to take care of minor home repairs.

And where had Phillip been? Chasing a woman not much older than Cassie, that was where!

The simmering anger flared to life again. Maybe if she had been a little less nurturing and a little more assertive, things would be different now. Leigh had never wished to be high-maintenance, but maybe she should have demanded a little attention.

Of course, it was all much too late to worry about it now. Water under the bridge and all that. Her chance to try and correct the problems with her marriage had come and gone.

"All right, I'll do it," Leigh said quickly, turning her thoughts from the bitterness of failure and regret.

"That's great. Ah, and here comes our other volunteer."

Leigh smiled and turned to greet the person she would be working with for the next few weeks. Her smile froze on her face, becoming brittle and false as the promises Phillip had made on their wedding day.

He was dressed in jeans, chunky boots and a plaid shirt. His hair was a little long and she could see the faint shadow of his beard on his lean, chiseled face.

"This — this is the other volunteer?" She turned to Brian. "Just exactly what are you trying to do, Brian?"

"Do?" Brian blinked but suddenly Phil stepped nearer and interrupted.

"I volunteered on Easter Sunday after I talked to the pastor. It seemed like — well — like something I need to do." Phil's brow was furrowed.

"Fine, good. Then you can do it alone, Phillip." She wasn't going to pretend any more. She hadn't wanted any witnesses to their difficulties, but this was too much. She simply wasn't going to act like things were fine. "I refuse to be manipulated."

Brian's face flushed. "I didn't think — I mean I didn't realize — How stupid of me, I shouldn't have asked you to volunteer, Leigh. I apologize. It will be all right. Phillip and I can manage the kids by ourselves They will just have to be restricted in wha they can do and where they can go. But i will be okay. Shirley will be helping out in couple of weeks. You are absolutely righ Please accept my apology."

Leigh's anger hitched up another notc

but this time it was on behalf of the children. Two restricted weeks — two weeks out of six. It would ruin their time in Tear Lake. It was selfish of her to make them suffer.

No, it was all Phillip's fault — again.

"I don't want you to think I'm ambushing you, Leigh. If you're uncomfortable —" Phillip began. So coming up here to ask for a divorce wasn't enough; he was going to insinuate himself into the remnants of her life?

"Ambushing me? Now why on earth would I think that? I don't like it, but I can work with you, Phillip. For the kids."

Brian's face was a portrait of embarrassed relief.

"Thanks. Now if you will help me round them up, we will get their nametags sorted and separate them into three groups so we can get them assigned to one of us. From that point on, each day from early morning until late afternoon when the youth group from the church picks them up to go to all the volunteer homes for the night, these children are our responsibility."

Leigh turned her back on Phillip with her heart pounding hard. She allowed Tim to take her hand and pull her to a cluster of blooming flowers. She erected a wall around her heart and promised herself that when

Phillip talked to her about a divorce she wouldn't cry. She wouldn't cry over him ever again. She intended to be strong; he was never going to see her vulnerable and needy ever again.

Some time later the kids were wearing bright blue and white nametags and had been split up into three groups of equal size. Brian outlined safety procedures for everyone, emphasizing to the children that they were never to leave their group leaders and go off alone. Many of the kids had been to Tear Lake before and nodded solemnly as he ticked off the rules on his blunt fingers. Finally they were ready to go exploring. Brian looked at his watch, gave everyone a time to return to the area and blew two short tweets on a silver whistle he wore around his neck. Each adult rounded up their group and set off in three different directions to a location of their choice.

"Flowers, flowers!" Tim yelled, and pulled away from Leigh. She had a moment of panic before she organized her thoughts. Quickly she gathered the rest of the group and caught up to Tim, grasping his hand to keep him with her. They wandered along the bark-padded trail, looking at flowers, birds and even a woodchuck, or whistle pig as the locals called it, who had come out to munch and sun. Hours later, feeling physically tired but truly exhilarated, Leigh finally delivered the children back to Brian and the members of the church. The kids talked a good talk but the signs of fatigue were on their little faces when the volunteer hosts gathered them to go to homes in Tear Lake.

Leigh had managed to avoid Phillip throughout the entire procedure. And not once had she had the impulse to hunt him down and shove him over a cliff. Maybe this would work out. His eyes burned into her back as she marched toward Gran's house, but she kept her pace steady and didn't even stumble once. The minute she was inside the house, she took the phone off the hook and put the deadbolt on the door.

"He can just wait," she said, swallowing the pain. She showered, slipped into old jeans and had a sandwich. Then she settled herself with a cup of tea and the little leather-bound journal. She smiled to herself. "This is really escapism literature."

*June 28, 1859*

Papa and the men dug with shovels late into the night. The flickering of their lanterns winking in the darkness made me think of angels sent by the Lord. I pray those men did not die alone and that God sent angels of mercy to them. At dawn they began to pull the first of the bodies out. Some of the men had wives here in the camp. They stood by white-faced, keening low. I was proud of my papa. He stood tall, though his skin was gray from fatigue and the dust of digging. He quoted from the Bible and I saw the words did give comfort. They are now burned into my heart, "Bow down thine ear to me; deliver me speedily: be thou my strong rock, for an house of defense to save me. For thou art my rock and my fortress; therefore for thy name's sake lead me, and guide me." Tomorrow Tear Lake will break ground for the cemetery. I'm sad. Since we came to this remote place I've felt so alone. But Papa has always said that any problem can be solved by God's word. So I've gone to Him in prayer and I'm reading my Bible nightly. I'm certain He will show me the right path.

# Four

"This way, Tim. Come stand over here by me." Leigh coaxed the little boy until he finally joined her, Phillip and Brian, who were sorting children in preparation for a morning walk. She avoided looking at her husband. So far she had managed to stay away from him. It was tense, but she was handling it the best she could. She wondered if he could still read her like a book — after twenty years it was inevitable, but maybe that sort of sixth sense went away with the love.

"Okay, kids stay with your leaders. We will meet at the church for lunch — and then we will do some rock skipping on the lake." Brian was a born supervisor. He grinned and blew on his whistle. A cheer went up among the older children who had been to Tear Lake before and knew that every morning the whistle blast was the signal for fun to begin. Tim smiled but he was quiet while he stared up at the mountain, all his attention focused on the craggy peak.

Leigh glanced up to find Phillip watching her. For a moment and truly against her will, she was swept back in time. They had met at a ski resort in northern New Mexico when they were both college sophomores. Her parents had still been alive then, before cancer took her father and a car wreck two years later had left her an orphan. Phillip had been the most handsome, considerate man she had ever met. She was the youngest, the baby of the family, and had secretly longed for marriage — for the kind of commitment her parents had shared. A whirlwind courtship and small wedding had been everything her girlish dreams imagined.

"Leigh?" Brian tapped her shoulder. She spun around. "You were a million miles away."

"Not a million miles, just a million years. Sorry." Heat climbed her face when she thought about her traitorous thoughts. She was ready to divorce Phillip. Now wasn't the time to recount happy times.

"I just wanted to tell you that Tim has a real curiosity about the old mining caves on the mountain. Don't you, buddy?" Brian ruffled Tim's thick thatch of hair.

Tim nodded and picked up the silver

whistle dangling from the red, white and blue lanyard around Brian's neck.

"I'll keep an extra special eye on him. In fact, I'm hoping that Tim will be my gentleman escort for the day. How about it?" She held out her hand. Tim released the whistle and took it with a smile.

"Okay, let's go." Brian led the way, followed by his troop of children. Then came Leigh with her kids and finally Phillip brought up the end. She had a mental picture of a goose with her goslings following along, or of the old train, each car in place, winding up the trail. The air was soon filled with chatter as the kids saw birds, squirrels and other small animals that called Tear Lake home. A robber jay flitted among them, flying so low some of the children squeaked and covered their heads with their hands.

"Pretty!" Tim shouted, pointing at the lake. Shimmering trout were leaping from the water, rainbow droplets sparkling in the clear air while they fed on low-flying bugs.

"Very pretty," Phillip said. Leigh turned to find him staring at her. Her group had been going so slowly that he had caught up to her. "But then I always thought you were the prettiest girl I had ever seen."

"I'm no girl anymore," Leigh snapped as

she ushered her charges up a pebbled path. His words were an affront. How dare he break her heart and throw her a crumb of a compliment. She wondered again what he was doing here. Why didn't he just spit it out and get it over with? Then another hurtful thought came to her mind. Was he bringing the new woman in his life to Tear Lake? Just the idea brought a bitter ache to her heart. Tear Lake was her place — her family had helped carve civilization into this wilderness; he had only inherited his right to be here because they were married. He had no right.

Leigh shoved him from her mind and encouraged the children up the path at a quicker pace in order to put some distance between them. She stopped so her group could climb a scatter of smooth, flat boulders. Tim was winded and a couple of the other smaller kids had red cheeks. Guilt flooded her. She was pushing them too hard in an attempt to outrun her rage and pain. The high altitude of the mountains could be tricky. Once again she was letting Phillip control her.

"Let's take a break." She made sure they were all settled safely on the flat rocks before she sat down. The morning sun had warmed the air. She took this opportunity to take off her windbreaker. The sun felt good on her arms beneath the short-sleeved blouse.

"Ouch," Tim said, touching one of the many Band-Aids the ER doc had put on Leigh's cuts. He leaned near and air-kissed her direction several times. "Make it all better." His expression was so serious her heart pinched a bit.

"Thank you, Tim." Then he snuggled closer so she could slip her arm around his shoulder. For a few precious moments they all sat in silence, staring at the lake below, entranced by the beauty and solitude of nature.

Suddenly Tim jumped up and pointed. His little body thrummed with excitement. Leigh followed the line of his finger and saw something sparkling and winking in the light. It was at the back of the church below them. At the same spot she had seen something sparkle on Easter Sunday.

"Go see it," Tim chirped. "Go see it, now!"

"Yes, I see it, Tim. But there are pretty flowers up this path. Let's go look at the flowers." Leigh thought she could distract him with closer wonders.

"Go see it." Tim was tugging on her hand. Now one or two of the other kids had spotted the sparkle and had joined in. Soon almost every child's voice was raised in plea to go and discover what was winking in the sunlight.

"Go see it. Go see it."

Leigh laughed. They were ganging up on her. "You little tyrants. So I guess you all think this is a democracy?"

"Mockracy?" Tim said, and the other kids looked confused. She was definitely out of touch when it came to talking to children.

"Do you want to go and see what it is?" she asked, feeling a little old. It had been a long time since Cassie was this small. She had almost forgotten the gently brutal force of a child's greed.

"Yes. Go see it now." Childlike voices yelled, the sound echoing in the cleft of the mountain and echoing down the smaller canyons nearby.

After much slipping, sliding and general good-natured horseplay while coming back down the mountain, the group made it to the church in excellent time. But unfortunately by this time a huge cloud had rolled in and shaded the entire lakefront. There was no way to identify the sparkling object now. Disappointment was written on every child's face.

Leigh swallowed hard. The knowledge of how much could hang on such a simple thing was clear in her mind. It meant a lot for these kids to find that flashy thing and solve the mystery of what it was. Funny how a discarded pop-top or a bit of broken bottle glass could look magical in the sunshine.

"I'll tell you what. Tomorrow when the sun is out, we will make a special trip over here and find what it was. Is that acceptable?"

After a quick discussion from within the group that had a smile plucking at the corners of her mouth, they all agreed. Even Tim. Leigh was relieved to be getting off lightly, but to be fair, she had to give credit to the appearance of the lunch ladies for saving her. They rolled up in a church van and started unloading sandwiches . . . what child could refuse a fruit cup?

The children were settled on blankets with sandwiches, fruit and juice boxes. Brian said grace and produced a worn Bible with fanned pages and a tattered cover. He read a few short passages to the children and then left them to eat. There was nothing preachy about it, just a quiet reading and a smile. She found herself smiling again.

"Come on, Leigh, this is the spot where we adults eat and try to catch our breath," Brian said cheerfully, nodding toward a round table with a gaily-striped umbrella sprouting from the center like a fat mushroom.

Leigh turned mulish. She didn't want to sit with Phillip. It was way too civilized to break bread with a man who was about to get rid of his wife in favor of a newer model like an old car that was no longer sleek and shiny, but she didn't want to make another scene in front of Brian and the children. So she swallowed her discomfort and what was left of her pride to take a seat across the table. If she kept her head down and angled just right, the umbrella pole would partially obscure her view of him.

Practically.

"I hope you will be at church this Sunday," Brian said, but Leigh didn't know if he was speaking to her or to Phillip.

"If you would allow it, Leigh, I would like to come over. I've something I need to discuss with you." Phillip's deep voice halted her breath. The food in her mouth turned dry and tasteless and she nearly choked when she swallowed it.

She leaned around the umbrella pole so she could look into Phillip's eyes. It was on her tongue to refuse, but she couldn't keep avoiding him or putting off the inevitable. She heard herself say, "Yes, there are things we need to talk about. And things that need to be settled."

He opened his mouth as if to say more but Tim came bounding up. "Find light," he said, his face scrunched up in concentration.

"What light are you looking for?" Brian popped a fat purple grape into his mouth.

Tim tipped his face up to Leigh. She could feel the excitement running through him. His eyes were round and it didn't take a genius to see he wanted her to interpret his excitement to Brian.

"We saw a flash of something when we were up on the mountain. Didn't we, Tim?" He nodded and clapped his chubby hands together. "I saw something in the same spot on Easter Sunday. I think it is at the back of the church," Leigh explained as she let Tim tug her up from her chair.

"Our time is almost up for today. There really isn't any way you can go exploring until tomorrow. I'll get the other kids organized." Brian began to sort children into two neat lines in preparation to be picked up by Tear Lake youth volunteers. It was left to Leigh to deal with Tim's obvious disappointment. He clung to her hand, trying to pull her away from the table.

"Honey, we can't do it today. We have to leave soon." Leigh braced her feet and tried to reason with him. He was having none of it and only tugged harder, his little mouth turning down at the corners.

"Tim, you have to let Leigh go now," Phillip said gently.

Tim frowned at Phillip and tugged harder on Leigh's hand. For the first time she saw a flash of full-out disobedience from him.

"No!"

"Tim —" Brian called. "Come on, buddy."

Tim dug his feet in and shook his head. Leigh didn't want to see this escalate but she didn't know quite what to do. Then Phillip crouched low and looked at Tim on his level.

"How about this? What if Leigh and I let Tim see what was shining in the sun and then we can take him to the youth office. How would that be?"

Conflict rose up in Leigh. She was happy to see Tim calming down, but Phillip was the last man on earth she wanted to go exploring with. Yet Tim nodded and smiled, reaching out to take Phillip's hand as well. Now the child stood between the two adults. Leigh hoped he couldn't sense the discord within her. She leaned close to Phillip and whispered, "This is a new low for you — using a child."

Phillip looked at Leigh over Tim's head.

"I'm sorry, I should've asked you first. But I'm just trying to help. Can we go look?"

She looked at Tim's expectant face. She told herself it was only for Tim's sake that she nodded. "If Brian hasn't got a problem with it, then I guess I can survive it."

Brian smiled a bit uncertainly, his gaze going from Phil to Leigh and back again like a man watching a tennis match. "Go ahead, just don't keep him too late; the family he stays with run a tight ship and are fairly strict about meals and bedtimes."

"Gotcha. Come on, let's go find a treasure," Leigh said, but it was Tim who led the way.

A mound of leaves left over from Tear Lake's long winter had blown up against the back of the church where large boulders hid them from view. Clouds were playing hide-and-seek with the sun, so it took a few minutes before Tim once again spotted the reflecting sunlight. Leaves flew in the air as he plowed through them. In minutes he was holding up his find and giggling with glee. A piece of red glass, oddly shaped with leaded edges, glittered in his hand. He turned it and angled it to catch the sun.

"Treasure. Treasure!" Tim yelled and pointed at the mound of leaves.

"Let's see what you have found, Tim." Leigh joined the little boy and dug into the leaves.

Phillip kicked at the scatter of moldering foliage. "I think there's more."

"More treasure?" Tim left the piece in Leigh's hand as he bent to help Phillip.

A lump formed in her throat as she watched them. Not so long ago this man had been the hub of her life. Now it felt like he was the enemy. Was that part of the problem? Had she been foolish to hang all her dreams on Phillip? She had an idea that Brian could probably quote a scripture that would answer her question but that would be too easy. She needed to learn where to look for answers. On her own.

"Looky, looky." Tim was hopping around like a kangaroo. Phillip was bent over something, brushing away dirt.

"What is it?" Leigh was surprised to hear herself ask, but then she was always a sucker for a good mystery.

"I'm not sure. It's broken and some bits are missing, but it looks like leaded glass — maybe an old-fashioned window."

Leigh bent near. Her heart did a little tumble when Phillip looked up at her. Sunlight glinted off his hair. She tried not to tear up when she thought of all they had been to each other and how much she missed him and how much he had hurt her. Anger threatened to swamp her soul, but she fought it and focused on the scatter of glass at her feet.

"It is a stained glass window," Leigh said, picking up one of the leaded bits of glass. "I wonder where it came from?"

Phillip shielded his eyes with the side of his hand and looked up. "Up there." He pointed.

Leigh tilted her head far back and gazed up. There at the apex of the roof peak, a small window had once been. It was boarded over now and, from the look of the gray, weathered wood, the boarding had been done long ago. The broken bits of leaded glass lay directly below it.

"Treasure window," Tim said.

"Yes, it is a lovely old window, Tim." Leigh looked from the boy to the broken window. She was struck with inspiration.

"Come on, Tim, help me gather all the pieces we can find." She dropped to her knees and moved the rubbish aside to get to the precious pieces of glass.

"Treasure." Both Tim and Phil bent to the task. Tim chattered happily the entire time.

Phil had the good sense to work in silence.

■ ■ ■ ■

Later that evening after her shower and a supper of tomato soup and an egg sandwich, Leigh curled up with the journal. At first she was distracted by the events of the day and her foolish heart pinching when the sun shone on Phil's hair, but soon it was all forgotten. The entries pulled her in and she was completely absorbed. The author was obviously a person of faith. Could that be the answer? Could she find the right path by reading the Bible?

The question nagged at her until she set the little journal aside. She picked up another book.

Not knowing where the answer might be she simply opened the cover of Gran's old, worn Bible and began to read at the first page.

*In the beginning God created the heaven and the earth.* Soon this book had all her attention. For hours Leigh read the story of creation, marveling at the power of the words. She read far into the night, telling herself that morning was going to come early, but knowing it and doing something about it were two different things. Like a child refusing to go to bed on time, she picked up the little journal once again.

*June 30, 1859*

The town is not like our old town. It is rough and loud and Papa says it is like a baby trying to grow. I like it. The train is more than eighty miles away so when the town needs supplies Mr. Gruber hitches up his team of big dray horses and collects the money and shopping lists from all the families. Then he picks one or two of the younger, single men in town and they make the long trip. I wish I could go but Papa says that wouldn't be proper. There are things young ladies cannot do. I don't like that. It is so unfair. Mama just smiles and says one day I will understand, but I don't think I will. When I have a daughter I am going to raise her differently — I swear it.

Leigh woke to the sound of a dog barking. She yawned and rolled out of bed, feeling as if she had just closed her eyes. Like a zombie, she pulled on her thick robe and padded down the stairs, her ears hurting from the dog barks. Now someone was knocking on the door — the knocks and the shrill yapping making a discordant rhythm. She scowled and grabbed the doorknob, intending to give somebody a piece of her mind. The air grew silent when she threw the bolt and opened the door.

Nobody was there. Suddenly a spate of renewed barking drew her eye. There, tethered to the railing behind the old oak rocker with the faded chintz pillow on the seat, was a puppy. His eyes glittered like dark jewels, and his tongue glistened like a ruby.

"Hello." Leigh went to the pup and squatted beside him, earning a face full of licks. "Who are you and where on earth did you come from?" The wriggling warm body nearly knocked her over before she could snatch the card attached to the back of his baby-blue woven collar.

"My name is Clancy," the card read in neatly typed letters. "Someone wants you to have my company."

"Hmmm." Leigh looked around but didn't see anyone. Who had done this? Brian? No, Brian would have knocked on the door and put the dog in her arms. Who else?

Had Phillip given her the pup? For a moment her heart did a little tumble and then the barrier her hurt had erected became cold and solid.

"Of course it wasn't Phillip. He is here to get a divorce so he can be free to begin a new life."

"Come on, Clancy!" Tim's young voice rang through the woods. Leigh had taken the dog with her and he had become the mascot of her group. Now the inner-city children had it all. Fresh air, beautiful country and a feisty dog!

He fit right in, snuggling and licking every child that came near him. And Leigh couldn't help laughing at how many times they returned for the same sloppy treatment. Her heart lightened watching them, and she was put in mind of the creation story and how God had provided such wonderful creatures for this world.

Brian tweeted his whistle and the children fell into a neat group with their leaders.

Today's activity was a fishing trip. Troops of smiling children with poles slung over their shoulder hiked up the steep trail. Leigh hadn't fished in years but she carried her pole and the tackle box as if she expected to land a whale.

"Remember the whoppers we used to catch up here, Leigh?" Brian asked, his face as flushed and happy as his young charges. Since they were all going to the same fishing spot the groups had merged on the trail.

"I remember the monsters I used to catch.

If memory serves, your catch was always a tad on the skimpy side," Leigh teased.

"I think you're mangling one of the Ten Commandments, Leigh." It was difficult to tell if he was teasing or not, but for some reason she didn't feel uncomfortable when he started talking about God. Maybe it was because of her late night reading. Maybe she was on the road to finding the peace Brian had and she craved.

*July 5, 1859*

His name is Rafael. He is an artisan. His English is not so good, as he says, but I'll teach him. Papa says it is permissible if our lessons take place in the church after service on Sunday morning. Mama and Papa will be there, of course, as he prepares his sermon since we still do not have a preacher of our own. We're having services inside even though the walls are not completely up. Mama and I clean the pews since the dust from the mines blows in. It will be a beautiful church when it is finished. I cannot wait!

# Five

Leigh smiled as she read. It was wonderful to see Tear Lake through the words of someone who had been here when it was founded — and it was wonderful to remember being so young and innocent. Had she ever been that young?

She turned the page, anxious to learn more about this sweet young woman but, as usual, the phone rang and interrupted her.

"Hello."

"Hi, sis. How are you?" Vivian asked.

"Fine, I really am fine."

"Well, you do sound better. What has been happening?"

"I'm doing some volunteer work with a church group. I get fresh air and exercise every day and I am so tired at night I am sleeping well again. This Sunday I'm going to church."

"That sounds wonderful. Anything new?" She didn't have to explain what she meant.

"Well, on Sunday — after services I'm meeting with Phillip."

"What? Phillip is there? At Gran's house? Oh, Leigh, don't tell me you took him back?" Vivian moaned.

"No. He is staying at a motel in town."

"Oh, for a minute there — Leigh, you're planning on divorcing him, aren't you?" Bewildered panic rang in her voice.

Silence hung on the phone line. Leigh knew her sister expected it — any modern woman with half an ounce of self-respect would expect nothing short of a complete break and a new start.

"I don't think that is the issue, Viv. I believe Phillip is here to ask me for a divorce."

"That low-down rat. Have you been in contact with anyone at home — I mean what about the other woman?"

"I haven't called anyone. I'm just too embarrassed. The last I heard she was divorcing her husband. I guess that means she and Phil are moving ahead — with their own lives, I mean. Look, let's not talk about it. Why did you call? Is everything all right with you?"

"Yeah, fine. Look, the reason I called was to tell you that I've done a search of our family records and so far I haven't found anybody with the initials CRT. There was a Cecelia Rose and a Caroline Rachel but they were both Reynolds. No letter T for either of them but I'm still searching. Any other clues you can give me?"

"Try looking around 1859 or 1860, and let me know if you find anything else?"

"Sure, Leigh. Sure. I love you, sis. Bye."

"I love you, too. Bye." Leigh rubbed her fingers over the three letters on the leather cover. She was anxious to read more of the journal but it could wait until tomorrow evening. Tonight another book called to her. So she changed into her softest nightgown, fixed a cup of cocoa and curled up in the chair. She picked up the old, worn Bible and started to read.

"What kind of dog is Clancy, do you suppose?" Brian asked the next morning while they waited for the children to arrive. Phillip wasn't there yet, so they were alone with one brave squirrel and the ever-present robber jay who flitted in a blue flash around the picnic area. "He is a smart little brute. Shirley and I are thinking of getting a dog when we get married. I wouldn't mind one as clever as Clancy."

"I'm not sure. What do you think?" Leigh asked, mostly to see if Brian would betray himself and reveal he was indeed her benefactor. Even though she doubted he had given her the pup, she didn't know him well enough to completely discount it.

"Collie?" he said and Leigh couldn't help but laugh. She was no expert, but the dog looked nothing like a collie. "Retriever?" he offered, frowning and tilting his head as he stared at Clancy.

"Like a golden retriever?" Leigh mused, looking at Clancy's chocolate-colored body and the thick curly waves across his back. "His color is all wrong, isn't it?"

"That's it!" Brian snapped his fingers in the air, startling the squirrel that had scampered near Clancy. "A Chesapeake Bay retriever."

"Why, I think you're right, Brian," Phillip spoke as he walked up, startling Leigh as much as the little squirrel who scampered back under a nearby fallen log. Leigh pressed her hand to her chest, not because of the fright, but because for a moment he looked exactly as he had more than twenty years ago when they first met.

"You were brilliant to be able to identify him," Phil complimented Brian.

"Aren't they supposed to have web feet?" Brian squatted down, patted his hand against his thigh and whistled. Clancy wriggled over to him and flopped over on his back, expecting a belly rub. Brian examined a paw. "Yep, they are webbed as a duck's. He's a Chessie, all right."

He picked up a stick and tossed it toward the lake. Clancy was up like a flash to retrieve it. "Give him a few more weeks and he'll be ready to put those webbed feet to use in the lake."

She was grateful the children arrived at that moment to distract them all. She was spared having to make small talk with Phillip, and her own traitorous thoughts were now occupied with the kids.

The day was one of those idyllic times that burns itself into memory and etches an imprint on the heart. Each new discovery brought wide-eyed wonder to the children's faces and Leigh found herself looking at creation through their innocent perspective. The three groups were mingled again today as they slowly made their way up the mountain, stopping to explore birds' nests, clumps of moss and lichen, or simply to watch the clouds drift across the blue sky.

"How could anyone look at all this and doubt God made it?" she said more to herself than anyone else. She was surprised when Phillip answered instead of Brian.

"I used to doubt. But since I came here I've been looking at most everything in a different way." He gave her a look that was unreadable, intense and caused prickles to crawl up her spine.

"I guess you'd call it a life-changing experience then." Leigh trudged up the pebbled path trying to gain a little speed so she wouldn't be walking side by side with him. He was confusing her too much. Phillip was here — but where was the woman he had left her for? She wanted to know. And if Phillip wanted to talk now, then there was no reason to wait until Sunday. She was bone-weary of pointless small talk as if they didn't have more important matters unsettled between them. So she said, "Phillip, would you come to supper tonight? There are some things I'd like to discuss with you. There are decisions to make, things to settle. I don't see any point in putting it off." She tucked a strand of hair behind her ear and waited for him to reply.

Phillip heard the words with only half an ear because the blood was rushing through his ears with a roar. He'd been doing a lot of thinking, and praying, since he had come to Tear Lake and attended that sunrise Easter service. Pastor Miller had been a great help. The sage old minister had been guiding Phillip, helping him to navigate the minefield he had made of his life — and Leigh's. He'd hoped for a little more time — prayed for it — thinking if he could just delay talking about divorce that perhaps they had a chance.

"Phillip?" Her voice brought him back. "Did you hear me?"

"Yes, yes, of course, Leigh. What time?"

"Come around six. We can talk after we eat."

And he thought, *A last meal for the condemned,* but what he said was, "Sure, I'll be there."

Phillip had been a lousy husband. He had never been there in the right way for either his wife or his daughter. Funny how he never realized any of it until the day Leigh packed her bags and left him.

With good cause. In fact, she should have done it sooner.

He kicked a rock out of the way and silently wished he could kick himself. He had messed up — big time.

Funny how all he had ever really concerned himself in twenty years of marriage was whether or not he brought home a good paycheck. Providing for a family was important — he knew that — but lately he had learned there was a lot more to being a husband and father than just a guy who paid the bills.

Funny how he had worried about his own entertainment, recreation. He had spent time, money and effort on lowering his golfing score and raising his bowling average and never once had he considered how Leigh felt about all the weekends and evenings he spent on bowling and golf.

Funny how he had justified his neglect of Cassie by saying she was a girl and girls didn't like to do guy things. She was a girly-girl and surely she wouldn't have enjoyed fishing or camping out. So he had never invited or included his pretty wife or his adorable daughter in his own selfish pursuits.

"Funny as a heart attack," he grumbled as he yanked a sweater over his head. He jammed his foot into a sock and followed it with a shoe. Then he repeated the process.

"What had Pastor Miller called it? — emotional distance — yeah, that was it." He'd kept his wife at emotional arm's length. He didn't know why — probably didn't do it consciously — but he had done it all the same. And then when the pretty young woman in his office had started coming to him in the break room and revealed her unhappy home life over coffee, he'd been ripe to succumb to the temptation.

At first he justified what he was doing by telling himself that he was being her friend — her sounding board. But inside he knew that wasn't true. Pastor Miller had helped him to face the truth. He'd known what he was doing, knew it was dangerous but he kept coming back for more.

It had been exciting.

He was flattered by her attentions. He cared little about breaking his wife's heart because he was having fun. Besides, Leigh was always there — at home — waiting — what she didn't know — right? Every man flirted a little — right? Every man had a right to a little innocent fun — right?

They had started going for walks during their lunch breaks, and then they met for coffee after work a couple of times a week. Then she joined the office bowling league and they were seeing each other socially a couple more times a week. She liked to play golf as much as he did. He found himself suggesting they meet and hit a bucket of balls now and then, so by then they were seeing each other at the office eight hours a day and almost that much after.

Leigh hated the golf and the bowling. At the time he was surly, indignant.

Soon he was spending a lot more time with the other woman than he was with Leigh. He flirted with her; she flattered him. He taught her how to improve her swing — she was grateful, giggly, told him how great he was. She told him how different he was from her husband and how his own wife didn't know what a great guy he was. She told him he was too young to be expected to be home, that he was vital, virile, needed someone to appreciate him more.

Yeah — right.

He had swallowed it all, hook, line and sinker like a fat, stupid fish with a little live bait in front of his nose.

And that was only the beginning.

They started exchanging E-mails, so even when they weren't together at work, they were only a few keystrokes apart. It was exhilarating. He lived to see her, talk with her, read her words on paper.

He felt twenty-five again. It was invigorating to be a man — not a husband or father — but a man.

On the hunt.

On the prowl.

With eager prey waiting for him to pounce.

He updated his wardrobe. He got a new haircut. He changed his aftershave. He bought an obscenely expensive sports car. He joined the gym and worked out — trimmed off every extra pound of fat, used a little of that hair-darkening stuff to remove the gray.

Even used the tanning bed.

She approved all of it while Leigh had been puzzled and confused. Leigh hated the sports car, the other woman loved it, said the wind in her hair made her feel alive. Leigh thought it was not very practical or safe.

He snapped at her, telling her he earned the money and he could buy what he wished.

"Yeah, I was really a big man, at my age having a young woman wanting to spend time with me. I thought I had outgrown my wife, that I was too young and vital to be married to Leigh."

Then the other woman told him she was filing for divorce. She would be free. The implication was there; all he had to do was give her a bit of encouragement.

And he did. God forgive him, he did. He more than encouraged her.

He listened when she talked about a future together and then he even began to think about it himself. It wasn't long before those thoughts became words. They talked about it together.

He was young — heck, he was in his prime — he was too young to be thinking about slowing down — nowhere near retirement, that was for sure.

Leigh was great. Heck, Leigh had been a great wife. She was the mother of his only child, but she wasn't as vital and full of life as he was — or so the other woman kept telling him, and he was more than ready to believe it. Hey, didn't every guy in Hollywood have a wife half his age? Wasn't it acceptable — even sought after? Wasn't it the true measure of a man to find a pretty young wife after he had made his career and raised his children? He knew half a dozen guys at work who had done it. They had made a nice settlement on their old wives and moved on.

Their ex-wives looked happy enough when he saw them out.

Yes, he found a way to justify every lousy, self-indulgent deed. He ignored Leigh so he wouldn't see the hurt and disappointment in her eyes. He even managed to convince himself it was her fault.

"What a fool. What a stupid, weak fool I was." Phil jerked a comb through his hair, wincing when he pulled some out. Then he forced himself to face his own reflection in the mirror — and his sins.

Yes, he had been ready to start a new life with this siren, who was close enough to Cassie's age to have been a friend of hers. She made him feel twenty-five again and that was all that mattered. He was working up the courage to tell Leigh he was leaving.

And then the bubble of lust and enchantment burst. The other woman's husband had found the E-mails. He had put two and two together and followed his wife. Phillip found himself in the middle of a nasty three-way marital meltdown.

But the guy didn't stop there. He found another way to vent his rage and pain. When Phillip got home that night, Leigh had asked him to explain a phone call that had come from the woman's husband. Phillip had been angry, embarrassed, and the words just tumbled out. Words that hurt and could never be called back. Words that suddenly changed his stupid fantasy into a horrible reality. She cried, broke things, put his clothes out on the curb for the entire world to see. Suddenly it didn't seem quite so romantic, or right.

His neighbors, people he had known since Cassie was a toddler, looked at him differently.

Phil no longer felt like a big man with a

young girlfriend. He felt dirty, guilty, and so sorry his gut ached with it.

Leigh walked out of his life. The world spun out of control. Phil couldn't breathe, couldn't sleep, and couldn't eat. He did go to work each day and saw the woman. But his vision must have improved because he realized with a sickening jolt that the woman he had been chasing had not been prettier than Leigh, she certainly wasn't smarter, and most important, she wasn't loyal, faithful or committed. In fact she wasn't even a pale shadow of his wife. But for a few stupid months he had clung to her every word. Like a lovestruck teenage boy he had resented any time away from her, dreamed of her, and anticipated seeing her again.

Right up until the moment his world crashed and burned.

Leigh was gone, and he had thrown away the most important thing in his life. But in the words of Tim — the singer, not the boy — he had given himself a long, hard look, and instead of going sky-diving or Rocky Mountain climbing, or hopping on a bull at a rodeo, he had come to Tear Lake in search of the only woman he had ever loved. He came looking for hope.

"Idiot," he told his reflection. "You may be too late."

He had risked, no, he had sacrificed, the most precious thing he ever knew — Leigh's love and trust — for the momentary excitement that a younger woman's attentions had given him. Pastor Miller had explained to him how lust in the heart was the same as lust in deed. He hadn't slept with her, but he had certainly conducted an emotional affair.

"So I've committed adultery even though I never took it that far," he admitted to himself in the silence of his motel room. "Thank you, Lord, for pulling me back from the brink. And I pray Leigh will give me another chance even though I don't deserve it."

But then, wasn't God's love all about undeserved chances? Nobody deserved the grace Jesus provided — it was given freely.

Now there was only one unanswered question in Phil's mind. Could he ask Leigh to hold off on the divorce? He was sure that was what she wanted to discuss. Could there be a tiny spark of love left?

"I pray there is, Lord. I pray you will touch Leigh's heart and give me a little time to prove I'm a changed man."

"Hello?" Leigh picked up the kitchen phone and balanced it against her shoulder while she switched hands and continued mashing potatoes for her dinner with Phillip.

"Hey, kiddo." Tom's deep voice came through the line.

"Hi. What's up?" Leigh poured in some milk and mashed some more.

"Oh, I just thought I should call. How are things?"

"Phillip is coming for dinner in a little while. I think he is going to ask me for a divorce."

"Whoa, you think he is going to ask you? What the — ? Leigh, he hurt you and betrayed your trust. Shouldn't this be the other way around? Shouldn't you be demanding a divorce from that unfaithful jerk?"

"I guess it doesn't matter which one of us gets the ball rolling. If it is what we both want — right?"

"What do you want?"

"I don't know anymore. But I do know I don't intend to be a victim — the poor long-suffering wife wringing her hands and snuffling into tissues while her husband has a fling to cure his mid-life crisis, and I don't intend to wait around and see if this madness that gripped him has worn itself out." Leigh was amazed that she could say all this aloud without tears or hysterics. "So I suppose divorce is the only option."

"Maybe you should —"

"Tom, I think I hear someone at the door. I've got to go. I'll call you in a few days. I love you, big brother."

"I love you too, kiddo."

Clancy was bounding around the kitchen, anxious for Leigh to go answer the front door. He was quivering with excitement by the time she set the bowl aside, wiped her hands on her apron and walked to the front of the house. She opened it, struggling to keep the pup inside, expecting to see Phillip; instead Brian was standing at the open door.

"Have I come at a bad time?" He bent down to pet Clancy, who flopped over to make the belly-rubbing easier. "I just got your message."

"Message?" Leigh's mind was a blank as she wiped her hands on her apron.

"Something about a window? Have you got another broken window, Leigh?"

"Oh, yes, no. I had forgotten all about it. I do have a broken window — sort of. I was wondering if you knew how to do leaded glass?"

"Sure. Are you wanting to put a window in here?" Brian squinted at the old-fashioned, bubbly, wavy glass in the windows of the front hall.

"No, not exactly. Tim and I found a broken window. I want you to give me lessons on how to repair it. I'll be happy to pay you," Leigh added.

"Hey, I like to show off my skills. When do you want to start?"

"When do you have time? I know you're busy with the children and your own business."

Brian frowned and pulled out a small book from his shirt pocket. "I can do it after the children are picked up on Wednesday, before church services begin. Will that work for you?"

"That will be great. Where do you want to meet? Do you have a shop?"

"Let's work in the basement of the church. There is a lot of room in that place. Only some old records are stored down there. Maybe I can persuade you to stay for evening services after we're done."

Leigh laughed at Brian's persistence in getting her to church more than once a week. "You have a deal." They were still standing in the front hall when Phillip knocked. She skirted past Brian to open the door.

"Am I early?" Phillip was ashamed to feel a little spurt of jealousy when he saw Brian.

He had no right to feel that way, but it didn't stop the green-eyed monster from rearing its head. But he tamped it down. After all, he was the last person who deserved to show any righteous indignation, no matter what.

"Hi, Phillip, nice to see you. So we have a date Wednesday evening, right, Leigh?"

"Right, Wednesday. Come in, Phillip. Dinner is not quite ready, the rolls have to brown," Leigh said as she closed the door behind Brian. Clancy hopped up and followed at Leigh's heels, leaving him at the door alone.

Another wave of guilty sadness washed over Phillip. Leigh was so formal, so tense. He longed to recapture the easy familiarity that had once been between them. How could he have ever thought that wonderful rapport was boring? How could he have ever looked at another woman?

"Is there anything I can do to help?" he called at her retreating back. She stopped and turned. Leigh's brows rose to her pretty hairline. Her soft brown hair was shiny and he wondered if it still smelled like her favorite freesia shampoo.

"You? Want to help with supper?"

"You never thought you'd hear that from me, did you?" Phillip tried to make a joke out of it, but his smile was weak. She was right to be surprised. In twenty years of marriage he had never taken the time to ask her that question. Leigh was a great cook — she had it all under control — that was the lie he had told himself to indulge his selfishness. But no more. He shoved up the sleeves of his sweater.

"I want to help. You tell me what to do and I'll do it. Lead the way."

Leigh didn't refuse. Instead she turned and walked into the kitchen. "Okay, if you really want to help. How about cutting up some tomatoes?"

"Whatever you want, Leigh," he said and meant it. He tackled the plump fruits with complete abandon. And what he lacked in finesse he made up for with enthusiasm.

"Now sprinkle a little seasoning salt over them," Leigh instructed, watching Phillip warily. For the last hour, her life had seemed surreal. In all their years together, she and Phillip had never shared this kind of simple intimacy. How ironic that now, when they were surely at the end of their dance together, they were finding this small equality. It was so bittersweet it brought a lump to her throat.

Leigh felt a little like she had as a youth on her first few dates. There was an awkwardness between them, as if they were strangers who didn't know the other's likes or dislikes, as if they hadn't greeted each other every morning for twenty years.

There was an anticipation of something unknown. Was this it? Was this thrill what had tempted Phillip? Was it simply that they had grown so accustomed to each other that the excitement of their relationship had turned stale? Or was it that when Phillip gave Leigh 100 percent of his attention, as he was doing now, a current of electricity arced between them, because as much as she hated it, she still cared? Is that what the giddy sensation of new love was all about?

It all made her unbelievably sad.

Phillip couldn't take his eyes off Leigh. Had he ever really appreciated her charm and grace? He had squandered their days together worrying about getting older and thinking of his own immediate pleasure. How many times had he played golf when he could've taken her hand in his? The sad truth nipped at his confidence, but then he thought of what he had recently learned about God and forgiveness.

It gave him hope. And where there was hope . . .

With a deep breath to steady his nerves, he made a silent vow. He was going to do everything humanly possible to win his wife's love and trust. And he was going to go down on his knees in prayer each night while he did it.

"Supper is ready, Phillip." Leigh was stiff and avoided looking at him.

"Great, I'm starving. Let me help carry this into the dining room. When we finish, I want to talk to you about something important."

*August 3, 1859*

Rafael said I'm pretty. Nobody but Mama and Papa ever said that to me before. My heart beats so fast when he is near me. I cannot think or breathe or swallow, my tongue gets all tangled up. And when he says my name, it is as if a tiny bird's wings beat inside me. I cannot let Mama or Papa know what I'm feeling or they would surely send Rafael away and not let me see him anymore. He gave me a pretty flower. It is not one I've seen before and I think it came from somewhere far up on the mountain. I've saved it by pressing it in the leaves of this journal. I'll treasure it forever.

# Six

The old-fashioned overhead light in the dining room cast a warm, romantic glow over everything. Leigh had not seen this side of Phillip since their college days. He was witty, attentive and charming. He was interested in her opinions. He gave her his full attention and regard. They made polite conversation, discussed the news and weather. They talked about the kids, the fish, the wildlife. They spoke of Cassie and her life in England.

They acted like awkward strangers.

It broke her heart.

And it forced her to admit she still had strong feelings for the man she had married. No matter how he had hurt her, her heart was not as fickle as his, apparently, for she couldn't banish the last twenty years of sharing a life together.

"Leigh?" Phillip lightly touched her fingers. "You went somewhere for a minute there."

"Wool-gathering." She jerked her hand back. He had broken her heart — broken their vows — she had to divorce him and move on.

Didn't she? Wasn't that the only option? If she stayed would she be weak and pathetic? How on earth would her family react? Or Cassie? Would she think her mother was allowing herself to be a victim? Would that influence the kind of man Cassie would choose? She didn't want to be a wimpy role model. She had tried to instill good values in her child, tried by example to demonstrate the way a woman should behave, act, think. Would Cassie see this as a cowardly act? Would she lose respect for her mother?

Phillip stood up from the table and jerked Leigh's thoughts back to the present.

"What say I make some of that flavored coffee you like and we eat dessert in front of a fire?" Phillip asked, wondering if he sounded as stupid and clumsy as he felt. Sharp teeth of guilt nipped at his conscience and tore chunks from his courage. He was weighed down with the burden of his own guilt. But he couldn't go back and change the past. He would if he could, but that wasn't possible. All he could do was move forward and pray that Leigh would or could give him a chance.

"That would be nice, Phillip." Leigh sounded wistful and detached as she rose from her chair and started to stack their plates.

"No, leave those for me, please. Go on, stoke the fire, I'll clear up and bring our dessert."

Leigh went into the living room and took out her confusion and frustration on the burning log. She jabbed at it with the iron poker, watching a shower of sparks fly up the old brick herringbone-patterned chimney.

Up until this evening she had been resolved — well, mostly angry, but a little resolved — to see her marriage end. Now she was simply confused. Her hurt had receded and now she carried a dull pain, like a toothache. But Phillip had been so attentive and kind and flirty that now she didn't know what she was supposed to do or say. She had been ambivalent and confused; now she was completely bewildered. He didn't act like a man who wanted a divorce — did he?

What did he want from her?

"Here we are, your favorite. I managed to get this at the bakery before I came, I kept it hidden because I wanted to surprise you." He held out a small plate of cheesecake. It was her favorite. Her hand was a little shaky when she took the plate and Phil went back into the kitchen. He returned a moment later with his own cheesecake and two mugs of steaming coffee, the hint of vanilla beans in the steam rising from the cups.

"Mmm, it smells delicious." She took a bite of the cheesecake but couldn't really enjoy the taste because her mouth had gone dry. She took a deep breath, gulped down the bite and looked Phillip straight in the eye.

"Phillip, I think we need to talk — about us."

He set both the cup and plate aside. "Leigh, I know you are right, but could I go first?"

*No,* she wanted to say. *No, you can't go first because I can't bear to hear the words and feel my heart break all over again,* but old habits die hard, and she heard herself say, "Sure, go ahead."

"Listen, I've been — that is to say, I'm so —" He stumbled over his words like an idiot. He took a deep breath and plunged on. "Leigh, when you left I woke up to a lot of truths."

Here it comes, she thought. The old

heave-ho, the final rejection. She didn't know what hurt more, the fact that he had betrayed her or this civil attitude he had managed to maintain all evening while he had planned to cut the final tie that bound them over cheesecake and coffee.

She just wasn't that sophisticated.

"I was an idiot, Leigh," he blurted out. "I was a damned fool." He stood up and came to her chair. He dropped down on one knee in front of her. "Please, Leigh, give me a little time. Don't divorce me. Not yet — not ever, if I've my way about it — but not yet. Please."

"What are you saying?" she managed to choke out.

"I'm saying I was a fool, a chump, an idiot, going through some stupid mid-life crisis. I hurt you — the most precious thing in the world to me. I'm sorry. I can never begin to show you how sorry I am — but I'd like to try."

Confusion swirled through her mind. A million emotions: relief, anger, hurt, disappointment and, yes — hope.

"What about — her?"

"Oh, Leigh. She is nothing to me. That sounds so trite, but I don't mean it that way. The woman was just some — some infatuation. I went a little crazy. I realized that almost the moment the door closed behind you. I told her what a mistake I had made."

"You mean she is out of your life?"

"Totally. I'll never see her, never speak to her. I sure don't even think about her. Can you give me a chance?"

Leigh stared at Phillip. She could see the truth in his eyes. The same kind of truth he had spoken on their wedding day. She wanted to say *yes, yes, I forgive you,* but the pain of his betrayal would not let her. She didn't think she had the strength to live through another disappointment like that. It had taken her too long to be able to get through the day without crying. Her own sense of survival kept her cautious. "I — I just don't know."

Phillip was silent for a moment and then he took a deep breath and smiled a tiny smile. "That is enough, Leigh. It's enough and a lot more than I deserve. I know that."

He stood up and gently kissed her forehead. "God willing, I'll be able to show you how much I love you. God willing, you'll be able to forgive me."

She didn't know what to say, so she said nothing. Phillip returned to his chair and for the next few minutes there wasn't anything but silence. Then Clancy bounded in and broke the tension. He nudged the table beside Gran's favorite chair and it tipped, everything sliding toward the edge. Phillip caught the lamp and the journal while Leigh righted the table.

"Whoa, that was close." He looked at the old journal in his hand. "What's this, Leigh?" She was grateful for his question. It gave them something neutral to discuss while her brain and heart tried to assimilate this revelation.

"I was up in the attic and I found that in a trunk. I think it must've belonged to a relative of mine."

Phillip frowned and ran his finger over the letters on the cover. CRT. "Nice leather work. Somebody spent a good bit of time on this. Funny, I don't remember anybody in your family with a surname beginning with T. Do you?"

"No. I've got Viv looking into it."

"Have you checked the cemetery?" Phillip asked.

"No, I haven't, and now that you mention it, I feel silly for not looking there first."

"What do you say you, Clancy and me go check it out tomorrow before the children arrive? I could swing by early and we could walk over together — if you'd let me, that is?"

Leigh was still a little unsure of this new

and improved Phil. But her heart still held love for him. Besides, she hadn't agreed to anything. She could call an attorney anytime she wanted.

"Sure, come by tomorrow. I'll make a thermos of hot chocolate."

"And I'll bring the croissants from that little bakery in town — the one that belongs to Brian's girlfriend," he said, rising to his feet once more. "I better go now. Good night, Leigh. Sleep well. I'll see you bright and early. And I know this is inadequate — but — thanks."

He was out the door and gone before she could say anything. Then she laughed aloud.

"Well, maybe he is not too new or improved. I see he left me with all the dishes."

When she was done cleaning the kitchen, she settled down in bed with the journal and the remains of her cheesecake and a fresh cup of coffee. She stroked the letters on the front lovingly before she opened the book and picked up where she had left off.

*September 12, 1859*

Winter is coming to the mountains earlier than I thought possible. Instead of the lovely red and gold leaves painting the mountain for weeks and weeks like autumn at our old home, they were a blaze of color for only a few days and now they are falling. It is like a snowstorm of color. Each morning there is more frost and the wind howls through the valley. The miners say we must harvest early and put as much food as possible in the root cellars that have been dug deep into the earth. Papa has gone into the mountains to hunt several times and the meat coolers are full. I'm afraid — not because of the weather, but because I've been told we will have times when the snow will be so deep we cannot go out of our homes. How will I see Rafael? How can I survive the whole long winter without seeing him, talking to him? I pray they are wrong and it will not be so.

Morning dawned in a salmon and gold display. The colors of summer on the mountain were sharp, the air crisp and clean. Leigh stood on the front porch watching Clancy chase a monarch butterfly around Gran's little garden of milkweed.

Leigh had risen before the alarm went off. She told herself it was simply that she hadn't remained up reading; she told herself she wasn't anxious to see Phillip, but deep inside she knew that was a lie. Her heart dared hope for a new beginning.

Phillip appeared down the lane. He walked down the path with sunlight glinting on his hair. The touch of white at his temples gave him a craggy, wise look. It occurred to her that he was not touching up his temples anymore and for some reason that small thing seemed significant. Then she brushed the thought aside.

Leigh told herself she was being silly — after all that had happened she shouldn't be so shallow as to notice what a fine-looking man he was — and she certainly shouldn't be so gullible as to think a little gray at his temples meant anything huge, but the fact was she did notice and she did hope.

Clancy ran to meet him and Phillip picked up a stick, tossed it into the air and laughed when Clancy caught it airborne.

"Clever pup, isn't he? Just look at the way he follows me." He reached the house with Clancy at his side. The pup appeared to be ready for whatever adventure might come his way. Phillip had a small paper bag in his hands and Leigh caught a whiff of fresh croissants.

"He's great company and I hate to disillusion you, but I think he would follow anyone with a bag of fresh baked goods. I just wish I knew who gave him to me so I would know who to thank."

"I'm sure when the time is right someone will confess to the dark deed." Phil chuckled. Then he looked at her — really looked at her — and she felt a blush climb her cheeks. It was silly for her to be awkward with the man she had shared her life with for twenty years, but her throat was dry, her heart was beating like a captured bird, and she couldn't think. To cover her tongue-tied confusion she called to Clancy.

"We have about an hour before the children show up. Are you ready to do a little sleuthing in the cemetery?"

"I've got the thermos of cocoa right here. Lead on, MacDuff."

Clancy ran ahead, poking his nose into flowers or leaping after iridescent-colored dragonflies, then he would notice the lagging humans and come racing back for them. They walked side by side, in no particular hurry.

"You look pretty today, Leigh." Phil didn't look at her.

"Thank you." She didn't look at him, either; she just kept focused on Clancy. It was foolish to take such pleasure in that simple compliment, but she did and she didn't want Phillip to know that she did. Her confidence had been undermined by what had happened. Hearing Phil call her pretty meant more than it probably should have, and she didn't want to let it cloud her judgment.

They reached the church and walked around the back and into the cemetery. Dew remained on some of the rough gray stones that lay in the shadow of the mountain.

"The older stones are toward the back, I think," Leigh told Phil as she picked her way through the uneven markers. Soon they were at the back row. The scatter of rocks from the slide Brian told her about lay very near some of the graves.

"The moss and lichen is thick on most of these. Can you make out the inscriptions?" Phil brushed dirt from the carved face of a brown stone. He squinted and read the inscription. "Horace Biggs. Father and husband . . . the date is too faint to read."

Leigh found a stone and crouched down in front of it. She rubbed her hands over the shallow cuts. "Mary something . . . O'Reilly, I think. That's all I can read." She moved to the next one. "Augustus Gruber, father, husband, teamster. 1870. I think I have heard that name somewhere — perhaps I read it in the journal. Maybe we are close."

And so it went for long minutes. Some of

the grave markers were badly weathered and only bits and pieces could be deciphered, but among them all there were no stones that bore a name that would account for the initials CRT. Leigh stood up and shaded her eyes from the sunshine. She looked at the scatter of boulders at the back of the cemetery.

"Brian said a landslide covered the back of the graveyard. Do you suppose it might have been on one of the markers that were buried?"

"We can ask him if they have any record of those older graves. Here he comes now with the children." Phil turned and gave Leigh a crooked smile. "Race you!"

Laughing like a carefree child, Phillip tore out of the cemetery. Leigh was shocked. This behavior was unlike Phillip, but then he had been acting like a different man. He taunted her with a wild whoop and Clancy tore down the hill after him. Leigh shook her head and refused to be caught up in their foolishness. She arrived at her own pace to find man and dog panting.

Brian eyed them both with amusement. "Well, I'm glad to see you're energetic today. We're hiking to the end of the lake for a barbeque and picnic."

■ ■ ■ ■

An hour later Tim was watching a group of children skip stones across the placid surface of Tear Lake. Clancy was leaping into the air at the edge of the water, barking furiously while the water skimmed at his paws. Youth volunteers from town had arrived in two Jeeps and were spreading blankets and setting up a portable barbeque. Several large plastic coolers had been unloaded, promising a feast.

"Children! Gather round." Brian hopped up on a crag beside a scrub oak and tweeted his whistle. "We're going to hike along the trail that runs to the south end of the lake. An old mine shaft is about halfway up the hill."

Excitement had the city kids nearly vibrating.

"Yes, I know, I know, it all sounds very dark and mysterious, but you're not to go too near. There are some tailings pits and other things that can be very dangerous. Nobody goes off without a buddy and then only with permission from me, Miss Leigh or Mr. Phil. Got it?" Brian was stern as he warned the children. One of the older boys had been staring at the weathered sign that hung on rusty nails from a gnarled pine post.

"Why is this called Haunted Trail?" He jabbed a thumb at the sign.

Brian grinned. "Well, that is a long story — one best told around a campfire after dark. And before you return to the city I promise you will hear it. But right now I want to make sure we are clear about the rules — has everyone got it?"

"Yes, Mr. Brian," they all yelled.

Leigh shook her head and smiled to herself. Brian was doing his best to sound mysterious about the trail's name. Truly the tale was more melancholy than frightful, but she had no doubt he would spice it up for his young audience.

"I think Brian missed his calling," Phillip whispered into her ear, sending a little frisson of warmth over her neck.

"What do you mean?" Leigh knew that Brian did a lot of witnessing to other people about God. She wondered if Phil was referring to that.

"He should have gone into the theater." Phil grinned. "He definitely has a flare for the dramatic."

"Okay, leaders. Keep a close eye on your children, but have fun. We'll meet back here in an hour."

"See you later, Leigh," Phillip said over his shoulder while he ushered his group up a worn trail. She heard him clear his throat and begin to talk to the kids. "This is a game trail. Animals use this to come to the lake to drink. If you're alert and quiet, you might see a deer or some other animal."

Leigh watched him while a lump grew in her throat. He hesitated and turned back to her. Then he waved. She wanted to trust him, but fear of being hurt again was keeping her cautious. Besides, she still didn't know how to forgive him. Was it possible to forgive such a betrayal? Could anyone really hope to do it?

"Tim, be careful," Leigh warned. She had taken her group to a little meadow she remembered from her childhood. Wildflowers grew in abundance and the wild grass was lush. When they arrived, they had been blessed to catch a glimpse of several elk bounding into the cover of trees. Now Clancy was plowing through the foliage scaring up birds, butterflies and spring midges. Tim was hot on his trail, laughing, stumbling and just being a boy.

"Children, come here so I can put insect repellant on your arms. And some of you still need your sunscreen."

Leigh spent the next few minutes armoring the kids against the biting critters. When she turned around, Clancy had disappeared. She glanced at her watch. They had half an hour to get back to Haunted Trail to meet with the others.

Leigh whistled and called, "Clancy. Come, boy."

The children soon joined her. Their voices rang through the meadow. But no answering bark followed. Finally, though she felt horrible about having to make such a decision and choice, she smiled at the children and said, "We need to get back to our picnic. Clancy will follow our smell. In fact, knowing his appetite, he may beat us back to camp."

"Race!" Tim sprinted ahead and the other kids joined him. Leigh was jogging to keep up with the tousled heads that shone like flags in the brilliant sunshine.

Soon the scent of grilling hamburgers wafted on the breeze. The kids seemed to gain speed and energy, but Leigh was winded and fell farther behind. She saw the kids burst into the clearing and blend in with the others. She bent at the waist, with her hands on her knees, trying to catch her breath.

"Leigh? What's wrong?" Phillip put his

arm around her and eased her to the clover-studded verge. "Tell me, what is wrong? What can I do?" He stood over her, his face wreathed in concern.

The apprehension in his voice touched her. When she had sucked a sufficient amount of the thin mountain air into her lungs and was finally able to speak, she did.

"I'm not hurt, just winded. The kids raced me — and have illustrated in no uncertain terms how old I am." There, it was said. She wasn't twenty, not even thirty-something. Phil needed to be reminded of that.

Relief flooded through Phil. He had been close to panic when he saw her bent over. It was a constant fear that he had squandered his time with Leigh and might not have a chance to be with her again.

"You're not old." He shrugged off the sting of his own conscience. Not long ago he had felt she was old — too old for a virile man like him. He might not have said the words to her, but he had said them to himself. Like so many other ugly chickens, another sin came home to roost. Shame brought a flush to his cheeks and a cold fist to his gut. He flopped down beside her on the clover, wishing he had the power to undo the past.

"You're not as old as I am." Only a few months ago, to admit that would have made him cringe. How stupid he had been to think that youth was the most important aspect of his life. And how could he have ever entertained thoughts of another woman — a younger woman? Leigh was so pretty with her rosy cheeks and bright eyes. There was a softness and femininity about her that only came with age and maturity. Perhaps all the clichés about aging like a fine wine were true. She shifted her position and looked back toward the mountain with worry written in her eyes. Then it hit him.

"Where is Clancy?"

"He ran off, the little rascal, and I didn't have time to keep looking for him. I thought sure he would show up by now."

"He'll smell the meat grilling and be back soon," Phillip reassured her, but he had his doubts. That dog had a good nose on him and the entire mountain should be bathed in the mouthwatering scent of burgers and frankfurters sizzling over charcoals. He didn't want to worry Leigh; she had grown so fond of the pup.

"Tell you what. If he isn't here by the time we're finished eating, I'll hike up the trail and find him. But I imagine we will be fighting him off our plates in just a few minutes."

She turned and gave him the kind of smile that melts a man's heart. At that moment he knew with a blinding clarity he wanted to be Leigh's knight in armor, even if it was a bit tarnished and dented.

"Thanks, Phil, I really appreciate that."

He jumped up and offered her his hand. She gazed at it for only a moment before she clasped it and pulled herself up.

His heart swelled and the flicker of hope became a tiny flame.

All through the picnic, Leigh couldn't shake off the feeling that something was horribly wrong. Clancy was such a smart dog, and though he was feisty, he was obedient. If he had been able to come when she called, he would have. Images of him being hurt assaulted her. Tired of trying to choke down food that had lost all its taste and appeal, she shoved her Styrofoam plate aside. Then she felt the warm, comforting weight of an arm around her shoulder. It was the most natural thing in the world to rest her head on Phil's strong shoulder. A little tremor of affection zinged through her body. When she realized what she was doing she sat up and jerked away. This was too quick and too easy.

"Shall we take a walk and find Clancy?" Phil gave her stiff shoulder a little squeeze.

"I'd like that." She cleared away her trash and tossed it into a mesh rubbish bin that was chained to a pole near the picnic area. They walked in silence. Leigh was tense, straining in case she might hear barking. When they reached the base of the mountain, Phil began to whistle. Leigh called and clapped her hands. They called until their voices cracked and their throats began to get sore.

Only the soughing of the mountain breeze answered.

"Let's go a little farther." Leigh was heartsick and couldn't think of leaving without finding the pup. Phil nodded and began to climb up the rough, rock-strewn path.

It was tough going and Leigh was soon out of breath. Every now and again Phil would pause and offer her his hand. Funny how well their hands fit together.

They paused on a rough shoulder of rocks. Once again Phil whistled and called Clancy's name.

There was no bark in reply.

Hot, unshed tears stung the back of Leigh's eyes. She called until her throat was dry, and still there was no sign of Clancy.

"He could still show up." Phil tried to cheer her up.

"It'll be dark soon." Leigh choked on her own sadness. "We can't look much longer. It is all my fault. I should have kept him on a leash."

"We'll call him all the way down the path. And I'll stay here tonight near the picnic area with a campfire going. If he sees a fire at the edge of the lake he'll come to it."

"I am not leaving without him."

"Fine, then we will both stay here tonight." Phil tried to quell the burst of happiness that decision brought. After all, he was worried about Clancy too, but he couldn't deny the thought of a camp-out with Leigh made him happy.

"Okay then." Leigh blinked back her tears and concentrated on the trek down the mountain. It was rough going at the best of times; now, with the blur of tears in her eyes and being tired from the day's activities, she was slow. Several times she felt the reassuring grip of Phil's hand on her elbow when she faltered or slid on an unseated stone. Finally they made it to camp. Brian was standing by one of the Jeeps. Everyone else was gone.

"No luck?"

"Uh-uh. The little guy is probably chasing a marmot or something. We're going to camp out here and hope the fire lures him in." Phil sounded confident.

"You're sure about that?" Brian frowned. "It might lure in a lot more than Clancy."

Phillip's jaw tightened. Leigh knew that look — it was his stubborn-as-a-mule, I-am-not-changing-my-mind look. "I'm sure. We're not going home with the pup still somewhere on the mountain. We've been living in the city for a while, but Leigh and I grew up camping out. We know the drill about four-legged predators. We'll be fine."

"Okay, but I'm leaving you guys the first-aid kit and a couple of sleeping bags that we carry in the Jeep. They aren't fancy, but they are clean. Oh, and you might as well have the leftovers too." Brian tossed out the sleeping bags and then unloaded one of the plastic coolers. Then with a chug and clank, he had the Jeep in gear and rolling down the hill. The circle of his headlights grew dimmer and dimmer until he disappeared from sight.

They were alone.

It was dark and cool, and Leigh felt uneasy. It was more than just the loss of Clancy; it was being with Phil like this. Now there was no buffer between them. Nothing prevented them from speaking openly about all that had happened. But did she have the courage to bring up the subject of their ruined marriage?

Frogs, crickets and night owls tuned up for their nocturnal concert. Leigh let out a sigh of fatigue, sadness and something else she couldn't name.

"Why don't you rest a bit, Leigh? I'll get us a nice fire going. Hey, look, there are a lot of leftovers from the picnic." He had the lid up on the cooler and was rummaging through the contents. "We're in luck. There are some dogs and a bag of marshmallows, too."

She eased herself down on a boulder not far from the spot where Phil was using stones to make a ring for the fire. Her legs were screaming. "How far do you think we hiked?" She rubbed her calf muscle and then untied her shoelaces.

"Oh, up and back, twice . . . I'd guess four, maybe five miles. You tired?"

"Exhausted, though I hate to admit it." She sighed.

Soon a fire was blazing, sending embers flying toward the velvety darkness of the heavens. There was only a sliver of a moon tonight and the diamond-like stars glittered overhead.

Phillip watched his wife with a sense of wonder and new discovery. She was lovely in the half-light of the campfire, her head thrown back, the smooth column of her throat exposed while she stared at the night sky.

He loved her. It was as simple and as complicated as that. He loved her. He had hurt her. He had betrayed her trust. He was willing to walk over hot coals to get her back, but was that enough? Could her tender heart ever trust him again?

"God willing." He murmured a prayer to the Lord. And there beneath the majesty of the heavens he believed his prayer would be answered.

Less than an hour later Leigh and Phil were sitting near the fire with marshmallows on long sticks. The scent of roasted hotdogs and fragrant pine smoke was a comforting perfume in the night.

"Wow, I'd forgotten how quick it cools off out here when the sun goes down." Leigh picked off the brown crust of her marshmallow and popped it in her mouth. The sweetness melted across her tongue.

"Soon as the sun slips behind the mountain it starts to chill. Are you cold?" he asked.

"Getting there."

"We should call it a night and get into those bags. I'll clear everything up and move the cooler far away from the fire, just in case any hungry bear invites himself for a midnight snack. After all my big talk to Brian, I had better back it up with some common sense, eh?"

Leigh watched Phil move in and out of the glow of the campfire. Her heart swelled with the same old love she carried for him, but she was wary, careful not to let her guard completely down with him.

"Okay, here you go." He picked up a sleeping bag, and after brushing away a few pebbles, unzipped the side and unfurled it on the ground.

Her bare arms were nothing but gooseflesh. She was anxious to crawl in and get warm but there were boundaries she wasn't going to cross — especially not with Phil — not now.

"Where are you sleeping?" she asked.

Phil gave her a look that she couldn't read. Then he banked the fire and spread the other bag out. "Right here on the other side of the fire. If you need anything, call out."

Leigh woke with a start.

"Shh," Phil said. "Don't move a muscle."

"What is it?" She stared at the stars overhead while every muscle in her body tensed for flight. Her heart was pounding. Some primal instinct kept her motionless.

What had woken her?

"I'm not sure, but don't move. No matter what happens you stay next to the fire and be still — and safe."

"But I —"

"Leigh, let me take care of you — please."

She heard the rasp of a zipper being drawn. Then she heard the soft rustle of fabric and the soft crunch of gravel underfoot. Phil was up. Suddenly the fire grew brighter and a shower of sparks entered her vision as they flew into the night sky. He was adding wood to the fire, building it up so it would grow bright and intimidating.

A noise from somewhere on the mountain reached her ears. It was the sound of limbs being moved, of dry sticks being broken.

Something was coming.

Leigh was torn between the impulse to get out of the bag and the urge to stay tucked up, warm and protected. It hit her then, that she felt safe with Phil. Here was the man who had broken her heart and destroyed all her illusions about their marriage, and yet she could not deny she trusted him to keep her safe.

A sound erupted from the trees behind them. Scrabbling paws tore through pine needles and leaves. Phil was braced with his feet planted and a big stick in his hand. And then something crashed into the open.

Leigh screamed.

Phil raised the big stick.

"Clancy!" He checked the motion in mid-arc as the dog leaped on him. Together they tumbled to the earth.

"Clancy, you scared me to death." He chuckled, rolling on the ground like a boy with the excited pup.

Leigh struggled to free herself from the bag, ending up crawling out of it to join Phil and Clancy. The pup was obviously as happy to see them as they were to see him.

"I thought it was a bear," Phil explained as the dog showered his face with doggie kisses. "What have you got here?" He pulled something free from Clancy's collar.

"It looks like a flower." Leigh took it from Phil's fingers. She held it near the fire. "I've seen this before, I have seen it —"

Recognition sizzled through her. It was the same as the flower she had found pressed in the old journal.

"I've never seen one quite like that. Do you know what it is?" Phil asked, scooting closer to her. They bent their heads together as Leigh examined it. His pulse hitched up a notch or two. This was true romance. Not some stupid infatuation, but true affection. The night air was crisp and clean and Leigh was right beside him. He wanted to pull her close, to beg her forgiveness, plead with her to let him move into the house with her.

But that wasn't fair or right. She had to make that decision and in her own time. This time — this time, he wasn't going to be a selfish pig.

"Well, since the prodigal pup has returned, what say we pack up and drive back to Tear Lake? I've got to admit that sleeping bag is not nearly as comfortable as my bed." Phil stood up and dusted himself off. Leigh watched him for a moment and then she stood as well.

"Yes, let's do that. I want to read more of that journal anyway. I want to know how the story ends."

*September 22, 1859*

It is cold. The valley is filled with smoke haze from our fires. I miss Rafe. His English is getting so much better and he is learning to write it as well. I'm glad I've this journal to record my thoughts. Winter is hard, everything seems quite frozen in time. There are no visitors, there are no new arrivals to greet and help get settled. It is just cold and the days are short. I miss

Rafe. I miss warm days. I wish winter was over and spring was here.

# SEVEN

Leigh walked down the narrow steep stairs into the church basement. Her face was tight and hot from the sunburn she had got today and her burden was getting heavy. Tim and Clancy had nearly worn her out; in fact, she had left the pup home so he and she both could get some rest. It was like having a healthy two-year-old to chase after!

The old building smelled a little like mildew and dust. She had expected something dim, but surprisingly the basement was well-lighted. One corner contained weathered wooden shelves that were stacked from ceiling to floor with old books and yellowed papers. A long table had been set up in the middle of the room. A roll of metallic foil, a soldering iron and various cutting tools were arranged with the precision of an operating theater. Panes of colored glass were stacked neatly.

"I'm impressed," Leigh said.

Brian turned and looked at her. "Hey, let me take that. I suppose it does appear a bit formal, but I've learned to have everything laid out. It saves time and wasted energy." He gently placed the box containing the pieces of the broken window in the center of the table. Then he slowly turned it on end and dumped out the broken window.

"Did you see Phil on your way down?" He flicked his finger through the glass, sorting by color.

"No, why?"

"He just dropped off this for you; I thought you might have seen him leaving." Brian handed her a small package wrapped in tissue paper.

She felt awkward. Not that Brian really knew what was going on between her and Phillip, nobody in Tear Lake knew, though she suspected he might have told Pastor Miller, and there was undoubtedly speculation since she was at Gran's old house and he was at a hotel. She took the package and stared at it.

"Aren't you going to open it?"

"Sure, sure." She tore the paper off and found a Josh Groban CD. There was a note too. She turned away and opened the folded paper.

"Leigh, if I wasn't a fool and had a way

with words I could tell you how I feel. But since you know I'm a fool, the best I could do was give you this. There is a song that says all I feel. When you play this and hear the words 'you're still you,' know I'm sending all my love and if I was a poet I would say it myself. Phil."

She folded the note in half and shoved it into her jeans pocket. He had simply signed it *Phil.*

"Do you have a CD player?" She held the slender case as if it were a precious treasure.

"Right over there on the shelf." He pointed to the shelves of books. Tucked away and covered with a fine layer of dust was a portable CD player. Soon she had it out and the mellow voice of Josh filled the room.

"Okay, where do we start?" She looked at the bits of glass and felt inadequate. Still, nothing worthwhile happened overnight.

"Usually we would be working from a picture or a drawing. I would trace the outline and decide what shape to cut the glass. But since we're going to be restoring your window, we need to work a little differently. First I'll cut you a frame from one-by-ones, and then we will see how many pieces we have to work with."

"Sort of like a jigsaw puzzle."

"Yes, just like."

For the next little while they worked in silence, the music playing in the background. Brian built a frame while Leigh tried to organize the hundreds of bits of glass.

"This is going to be a big job."

"It is. In fact, I'd suggest you find a partner. This is going to be slow going. The more help you have, the quicker it will go."

At that moment the song on the CD caught Leigh's attention. She heard the phrase "you're still you," just as Phil had said. She listened to each new word while a lump grew in her throat. If Phil really shared those sentiments then he did love her, but if that was true, then his actions were even harder to understand.

If he loved her before and betrayed her trust, could he do it again? She tried to push the questions to the back of her mind while she worked on the bits and pieces of the stained glass window.

Time flew by, and before she knew it the CD had played through and Brian was rubbing the back of his neck.

"I'm ready to call it a day, how about you, Leigh?"

She glanced at her watch and felt the flush

of embarrassment climb her cheeks. They had been working for nearly three hours.

"Oh, Brian, I didn't realize it was so late."

"No problem, but I need to grab some dinner."

"You haven't eaten? Now I feel even worse."

"I hurried to services and forgot to grab something." He cleared up the rest of his tools. The broken stained glass window now had a wooden frame. He had even managed to connect some of the edge pieces. It looked very much like a jigsaw puzzle, a large one, with many missing pieces. *A little like my life,* Leigh thought.

"You're coming home with me and I'm cooking you dinner. It is the least I can do." Leigh went to the CD player and popped out the disc and put it in the plastic sleeve. Her toe caught on something and she bumped a shelf. A stack of books and an entire section tumbled down at her feet. Her gaze was drawn to a handwritten date.

"Are these Tear Lake's records?" She bent down and grabbed several pieces of paper.

Brian walked to the shelf and squatted beside her. "Yeah, I think." He picked up a page and looked at it. "Uh-huh. These are the birth and death records kept by the church. Why?"

"I've been looking for an ancestor of mine but haven't had any luck. Do you think I could borrow these? I promise to be careful and return them in good condition."

"I'm sure Pastor Miller doesn't mind. In fact, I bet he would jump at the chance to have someone clean up this mess. Go ahead and take them — in fact, if I'm coming to dinner the least I can do is carry them out to my truck. Do you need a ride?"

"I did walk over."

"Even though this is Tear Lake and our crime rate is a negative number, I don't think you should walk home alone. So let's load these and I'll give you a lift."

Leigh and Brian walked out of the church and into the night. The moon was full overhead, casting a silvery sheen to the landscape. Brian was headed toward his pickup when a man stepped out of the shadows. It was Phil.

"Phillip, what are you doing here?" Leigh was a little flattered, even though she told herself that was stupid.

"I was waiting for you. I was hoping I could walk you home."

Leigh glanced at Brian. He had loaded the stack of old books into the cab of the pickup and was obviously doing his best not to eavesdrop.

"Sure, why not? Brian, I'm going to walk with Phil. The house is unlocked. Go ahead and let yourself in — and don't let Clancy annoy you. There is soda and iced tea in the fridge. We will be right along, and I will get you fed."

Brian waved and hopped in his truck. As soon as he was around the bend in the road, the night sounds returned and the semi-darkness settled over them like a blanket. Crickets chirped and the sound of owl's wings fluttered overhead.

"This is nice," Phil said, slipping his hand into Leigh's. She didn't object and he took that as encouragement. "Leigh, I wanted to talk to you." He felt her tense beside him. For a moment he was swamped with guilt, but he fought it off. He would never succeed in earning Leigh's trust if he allowed himself to be pulled back into the paralyzing shame of old sins. He had to keep putting one foot in front of the other; after all, Leigh's heart and love were at the end of the path. She was worth any amount of pain.

"I wanted you to know I've made an important decision, Leigh."

"What is that?"

"I'm being baptized this coming Sunday."

She stopped walking and stared at him with a mixture of disbelief and curiosity.

"Really?"

They started walking again. "Yes. I'm a new man, Leigh, born again in Christ's love. He has forgiven me all my sins. For years I've had it all wrong, Leigh. I put myself first above everything. But now I understand. God first, and then He will put everything else in its proper place. Will you come?"

"Sure. I'll be there." They had reached Gran's house. The soft yellow glow of the bug light on the porch was inviting. "Hey, where is Brian's truck?"

"Maybe he parked in back," Phil said.

Leigh opened the front door and stepped inside. She flipped on the lamp near the front door. "Nope, here are the records he brought home for me. Oh, here is a note. He says he is having dinner with his fiancée. There is some crisis at the bakery. I guess we're on our own."

Phillip's heart swelled with love each time he looked across the dining table at his wife. He had fantasized about the small blessing of having a quiet meal with her. The reality far outweighed his hopes. They had shared stories of the kids, laughed over small incidents, even did the unthinkable by feeding Clancy a nibbly or two from their plates.

It had been warm, wonderful, and he never wanted it to end. Phil watched her over the rim of his cup while he sipped his coffee, not in any hurry to have this evening come to an end.

"Mmmm, this is good. You always make the best coffee."

Leigh tried to balance her feelings while she smiled at his compliment. Every time Phil said he wanted to talk, she expected it to be about finalizing their separation, talking with an attorney and getting a divorce, but then she would check herself. She believed him when he said he wanted another chance. She just had to find a way to trust him — and that was the nut of her problem. Her heart wanted one thing, while her head cautioned against it.

"Okay, Phil, we are all done and we have talked about everything under the sun, but you said there was something you wanted to talk about?"

She braced herself for the worst and was stunned when she heard him say, "I'm thinking of selling my car."

Leigh's brows rose. "Your sports car?" The car had been a bone of contention. She winced when she remembered the harsh words and heated discussions that had followed its purchase. When he brought it home without even consulting her before the purchase, she had been hurt, feeling left out and insignificant in Phil's daily life. She had vented her frustration, but now in retrospect she realized that the car symbolized her denial about her disintegrating marriage and Phillip's desperate yearning to remain young.

"Yes. I know you've always hated it." He paused before adding, "And with good reason."

"I liked the little horse on the emblem, but beyond that I can't deny I don't like that car, but if you're selling just because I hate it —"

"No, I'm doing it because it was a stupid thing to have bought in the first place. It is small, expensive and a completely ridiculous shade of red, and owning a convertible at my age is dumb. It is definitely the kind of car a man in a mid-life crisis would own. I'm no longer that man. I may be in mid-life, but thanks to God, I'm not in crisis. I'm trying to change things, Leigh — change myself."

"Okay." Leigh didn't know what to say to that — because those had been exactly the reasons she hated the car, and though she had loved Phil unconditionally their entire marriage, she couldn't deny there were things about him she would definitely change if she could.

But wasn't that terrible?

She'd never agreed with people who married someone and then set out to remodel them. A hot conflict of emotions rose up inside her. Was this nearly the same thing? He was asking her not to divorce him, but if she was thinking they could start again and she would change him — it seemed like a recipe for failure.

"Besides, I've something special in mind to do with the money." His words broke into her thoughts. She set her cup down on the table and toyed with the brocade pattern on the linen tablecloth, unable to look at him.

"Buying one of those big SUVs with the dark windows? Those seem to be almost as popular as convertibles," Leigh quipped. She should have felt a stab of guilt for being snippy, but the truth was, she didn't. Deep down inside she was still angry, and from time to time it bubbled over. She was working on forgiving him, but it wasn't going to be overnight.

Phillip smiled. "I've missed your wit." He chuckled, taking no offense. "I'm going to give the money to Brian for his kids' summer program."

Leigh stopped rubbing the outline of a tea rose. She stared at Phillip. She tried to wrap her mind around what he had just said, but it was difficult. On the outside he was the same: handsome, rugged, strong stubborn chin, the same warm, brown eyes. But inside he was a man she didn't know. She liked this new man very, very much. When she acknowledged that, a bit of her lingering conflict crumbled and fell away.

He stood up from the table suddenly. "Hey, you reheat our coffee while I toss a new log on the fire. Then maybe you and I can start looking through those church records to see if we can find you an ancestor with the initials of CRT."

*October 10, 1859*

Rafael has decided he will try mining. His lovely hands were not meant to grub in the rock until they crack and bleed, but I cannot budge him. He says it is for us. He says when he makes his fortune he will speak to Papa. He says this is America and here he can become a man of property. He says I must understand this and not worry because it is the way things must be done. How will I wait when my heart beats with love?

*October 27, 1859*

The first real snow came today. It is not light and fluffy like the snow back home. This is a snow with icy teeth in it. It blows and cuts. It sweeps through the valley below the mountain like a giant's hand. Now ice lies in thin sheets on the streets and on the roofs of the houses. Only the chimneys and stovepipes are free of it. Mr. Gruber's dray horses were pulling a load and fell today. My heart was in my throat, but thank the Lord, the big geldings' legs did not break. I already hate the winter here.

# EIGHT

"The scene is really starting to take shape." Brian held the soldering iron at the ready while Leigh fitted another piece of the window in place. They had managed to salvage the entire top and were slowly working their way down. A sunrise in yellow and red glass blazed across the top beneath the new wooden frame.

"It is lovely. I can't wait to see what the entire thing looks like." Leigh had learned how to cut the glass, foil it and add the lead strips. Now she was learning the process of soldering the joints to give it strength. At the end of a long day of laughter and exploration with the children, this was a quiet respite. In some ways it was very mundane work and her mind was free to skip along on autopilot while her hands reassembled the mysterious glass puzzle.

"Are the rugrats looking forward to the

hide-and-seek game tomorrow?" Brian asked.

"Are you kidding? That's all they could talk about. Especially Tim. If not for Clancy, I don't think I could keep up." She laughed and focused on the joint of lead. Just a light touch of the hot tip of the soldering iron and it would be fused.

"I hope it is not too difficult for you to take part of Phil's group tomorrow."

The tip of the soldering iron slipped. "Ouch!" Leigh burned her finger.

"You okay?" Brian took the soldering iron from her hand.

"Yeah, it is nothing. Why are you splitting up Phil's group?"

Brian's expression slipped. "Phil has gone back to the city. He said he had some business to take care of. He got a phone call from some woman. He said it was personal business."

Leigh's heart froze. Just like that, all the hope and trust that had been kindled died inside her. She was sure it was the woman he had been pursuing. A part of her brain went numb with pain. But then she sucked in a deep breath. Phil wasn't that man; he had changed. Could she change too? Could she set aside the bitter suspicions and treat Phil like the new person he was becoming?

"Leigh, you look upset." Brian handed her a tube of antibiotic ointment for her finger. "I shouldn't have said anything, should I?"

She took it and squeezed a soothing glob on the red tip of her finger. "For a moment I jumped to a conclusion, but I don't want to do that. I don't want to prejudge him."

Brian smiled. "That's what Jesus would do."

"What?"

"He would not judge. I'm proud of you, Leigh."

She smiled back and said, "Me too." Maybe Phillip wasn't the only person needing to change. Perhaps she needed to change and seek forgiveness too.

"Oh, Clancy, you didn't!" The pup had discovered the bliss of chewing shoes. He had destroyed one each of three different pairs. "You little monkey, couldn't you have just eaten one entire pair?" Leigh scooped up the ruined footwear and tossed them into the trash. She had gone to the market and bought him two big rawhide twists, hoping they would keep him busy. In the meantime, she was putting all her remaining shoes at the top of the closet. She was on her tiptoes putting her favorite pair of slings on the shelf when an old yellowed envelope fluttered down. She picked it up and opened it. Inside was one of the pressed flowers like the one that had been in the journal.

Where did this bloom come from? How strange it was that she had never seen the flower before and suddenly it kept turning up. First the one pressed in the journal, then Clancy had a fresh one in his collar, and now she'd found one in Gran's closet.

She pushed the thought from her mind and turned her attention to Clancy, who was whining. He was ready for a short walk. The sunset was glorious and fingers of salmon drifted on the surface of the lake. She unsnapped his leash and let him run free. When he finally returned to her, his feet were damp and his tongue lolled out the side of his mouth in a happy canine grin. She knew he was ready to go inside.

Leigh fixed herself a cup of tea and settled down with her gran's worn Bible. She read until, as usual, the phone interrupted her. She expected it to be Tom since he hadn't called for a while, but when she answered, it was a woman's voice on the other end.

"Hey, can I talk to Phil?"

The voice was chirpy, young, and it sent a shaft of pure dread lancing through Leigh. "No."

It was on her mind to just hang up but she took a deep breath. "He isn't here, can I take a message?"

"Just tell him he left his coat at my place. This is Tammy."

Leigh placed the phone in the cradle and sagged into a chair. She had begun to trust again. Now she was at a crossroads. Somewhere in the back of her mind she knew that she could choose to trust, or she could allow the last brick to be fitted into the icy wall of self-protection that surrounded her heart.

"What should I do?" she said aloud. And then Leigh realized she wasn't talking to herself. She was talking to God. She closed her eyes, bowed her head and began to pray.

An hour later Leigh was putting a new log on the fire to take the chill off the house. A spring storm was blowing in and the weatherman was predicting an inch of snow in Tear Lake. She loved the unpredictability of the mountains. It was one of the things she had missed the most when she was living in the city.

It occurred to her that Phillip had changed a lot since he had accepted Jesus, but she was changing too. Maybe she hadn't stood up and professed her faith but it was growing nonetheless. She found God was in her mind much of the time and prayers slipped from her lips quite often. At night before she went to sleep she said prayers for Brian's city kids, and her own daughter far away in England.

"And for my marriage." She prayed nightly that God would work in her life and show her the path. Was that why she trusted more?

Clancy leaped to his feet and growled low in his throat. A light knock on the door prompted a furious spate of barking. Leigh closed the Bible and went to the door.

"Who is it?"

"It's Phil."

Leigh opened the door. He was standing in the glow of the porch light with his hands behind his back. A crooked half-smile quirked his mouth and he looked much as he had twenty years ago when he had won her heart.

"Come in," Leigh said. She was tempted to demand answers about why he had gone to the city and whom the woman was that called. But she tamped down those questions and opened the door wide. It was symbolic of the door she had just thrown open in her own heart.

"I've a surprise, Leigh. Ta-da!" He brought a huge bouquet from behind his back. It was white roses and lilies. The fragrance was sweet, inviting her to bury her nose in the blossoms and inhale.

"They are lovely, but what is the occasion?"

"We're celebrating, honey." He leaned close and placed a quick kiss on her cheek.

"I need to put these in water." She didn't want to destroy this moment, but the time was long gone for her to pretend and look away. She forced herself to tell him. "Phil, a woman called here for you. She said you left your coat at her place."

He looked puzzled. "I did? Huh. I guess I was just so distracted —" He looked at Leigh and a frown appeared. "What? Leigh, what's wrong?"

She shook her head. This new ease between them was fragile and tenuous. She didn't want to break it but she knew they couldn't have a new start without total honesty. "When she called I thought it was . . ."

"Oh, Leigh. I told you that was over and it is. You can trust me. I swear it. I left my coat at a young woman's house for all the right reasons." He reached inside his shirt pocket and pulled out an envelope. "She was young, perky and rich."

Leigh opened the envelope and pulled out

a bank cashier's check. The number of zeros was truly staggering. "Is this what I think it is?"

"Well, if you think it is the proceeds from the sale of my sports car, you're right. I hope you like what I got us."

"Us?"

He stared into her eyes. "Yes, for us, Leigh. I got us a small pickup. It is a lot more practical here in Tear Lake. We can cut wood and carry Clancy — with one of those safety harnesses, of course."

Leigh's eyes welled with tears. Her hands were shaking when she slid the check back into the envelope. Phil slipped his arm around her waist. Then he grinned and said, "Hey, how about a cup of cocoa? Then I'm itching to get back into the journal."

Her heart swelled with love and the barometer of her trust hitched up a notch. Phil was winning her back.

A short while later Leigh and Phillip were on a quilt on the floor; they had their heads together while they read the little journal. Time was suspended. When the room grew cool, Phil hopped up to put another log on the fire.

Clancy decided he needed to go out so Leigh put him in the backyard. When she returned Phil was sitting up, one elbow propped on his knee.

"Come sit by me," he said softly.

And Leigh did as he asked. She pulled a pillow off the sofa and scooted near to him. It felt so right to sit side by side before the roaring fire. Without being conscious of doing it, she suddenly found her cheek leaning on his strong shoulder.

"Read it aloud, Phil."

The journal was revealing an old story at the same time it was bringing them back together.

*October 29, 1859*

The snow has fallen for a day and a half. I cannot go out except to the privy and that is a horrible experience! Papa has strung a rope from the back door of the house so we can hang onto it, but still I'm frozen by the time I get back. The only nice part is that I've more time to write in my journal. I rubbed some of the frost off the window today and I saw Rafael. At least I think it was him. All the men are bundled from head to toe but the man paused and raised his gloved hand to me. I miss him so. I wonder how long winter lasts here?

# NINE

"The Lord has answered my prayers. I don't know what to say, Phillip. You have no idea what this money will mean." Brian's voice had gone husky with emotion. "For years Shirley and I have talked about finding the money to build a center with a dormitory and a kitchen. We've been saving on our own, but it is slow. The bakery always needs something — a new oven or the roof repaired — but if we have the facility we could bring children from the city for more than just six weeks."

"I'm glad it helps." Phil was feeling awkward and embarrassed. He had never done anything like this before — never even thought about it. His secretary brought the year-end pleas for donations to him each year, and on advice of his accountant he had answered most of them for tax purposes. The spirit of giving had never been present until now. He had a lump in his throat and a warm feeling in his heart. And the fact that Leigh was looking at him with something like admiration in her eyes didn't hurt either. His warm heart beat a little faster.

"God bless you, Phillip."

Brian's smile was thanks enough, but when Tim ran up and flung his arms around Phil's waist he felt like he grew four inches. This was what bliss must feel like, he thought.

"Come, throw ball. Throw ball. I can catch," Tim said.

Brian laughed and folded the check to slip it into his wallet. "I want to announce your donation to the town at the Founders' and Newcomers' Festival next week. But now we need to have fun. Isn't that right, Tim? We have a baseball game to play. Let's separate the kids into two teams. Today it is home runs for everyone!"

"What do you think, Leigh, home runs?" Phil slipped his hand in hers while Tim grabbed on to the other.

"At least one each." She laughed and the sound washed over Phil. Then to his delight, she tugged down the bill of his baseball cap and said, "Race you to the field." She laughed and took off with Tim at her side.

He loved this woman.

■ ■ ■ ■

"Run, run!" Leigh yelled. Her voice made Phil reach deep inside. He was carrying Tim in his arms and Clancy was running right beside him, barking furiously as they attempted to make the last run of the day. So many kids had hit home runs that some of the smaller ones had tired out. Brian and Phil had taken turns running them around the bases. He was happy but exhausted as he shot across home base. Tim was giggling when Phil set him on his feet and collapsed. He expected to be slathered with dog kisses but Clancy wasn't there. In fact, he realized that suddenly it was quiet; the dog wasn't barking.

"Clancy?" he called. He had grown just as fond of the little beggar as Leigh. There was a flurry of activity as the volunteers from town came to collect the children from the ball field. A careful count of heads was done twice and then Brian supervised their departure. After the kids were gone, Phil saw Leigh whistling and calling for Clancy. He made his way through the tall grass to the spot where she was standing on a boulder.

"Did he do it again?"

"Yes, and this time it is my fault. I never should let him off the leash if he is going to be running off."

"The little beggar is probably chasing rainbows." Clancy's frequent disappearances gave him the opportunity to take long, private walks with the woman he loved. Being alone with Leigh in the midst of God's beautiful mountains wasn't anything short of miraculous. Today he hoped to make another small step back into her heart.

They walked up a faint trail that wended its way through tufts of grass and columbine spikes. The days were growing longer; daylight savings time was only a few weekends away. Then it would be summer with its golden sunshine and long, long days.

"Phil, I'm proud of you. I know how much that car meant to you."

He chuckled but there was little humor in the sound. "Actually, Leigh, I found out how little that car and every other material thing mattered to me when you left. I hope I've learned how to value what is really important. Like you."

Leigh felt a blush climbing her cheeks. How silly it was for her to stammer and blush with shyness each time her husband of twenty years spoke of loving her. She was growing weary of her own mixed emotions.

She wasn't a girl anymore. It was time to start dealing with her feelings like a grown woman.

"Leigh, I wanted —"

"Phil, I was hoping that —"

They laughed when they both spoke at once. A small runnel of water blocked their path and Phil picked Leigh up by the waist and swung her over.

"My hero." She giggled.

"You don't how much I wish that was true," he muttered to himself. It is now or never, a voice inside Phil's head prompted. "Leigh, I was wondering if —"

"Phil, before we go any farther, there is something I would like to ask you."

"Shoot."

"Are you planning on staying in Tear Lake?" She couldn't believe she had asked. Though the question had been in her mind for some time, she had fought asking.

Phil stared at her for a long minute. His expression was taut; every muscle in his shoulders was tense. Finally he said, "I think that depends a lot on you, Leigh. I've made no secret of the fact I intend to do everything in my power to see us reconciled — to see our marriage put back together. Is there a chance that can happen?"

This new Phil was still surprising her. The

old Phil would never have been so direct. He would have hemmed and hawed and danced around the issue. That had been part of their problem; they never openly discussed things. But this new version of her husband was a man of candor. He deserved no less from her.

"There is always a chance, Phillip." She turned away before the flush of embarrassment reddened her cheeks.

Phil halted in his tracks. This was more than he could hope for. He was going to ask Leigh if he could come pick her up every morning. He hurried and fell into step beside her.

"Are you busy tonight, Leigh? If not I would like to take you to dinner. And then maybe I could help you with the window?"

"I'd love to go to dinner. And I'd love to have some help on the window."

Phil smiled. Leigh was more forgiving than he could have hoped — more forgiving than he had any right to expect. "Good, I'll swing by Gran's house and pick you up —"

"Listen! Do you hear that?" Leigh heard the sound of far-off barking.

"It's coming from over here." Phil led the way up the mountain. A small path lay between a rock face and scattered boulders.

Finally they reached a flat meadow. A landslide of rock scarred one side of the canyon. And there among the treeless pale stone fan was a tiny, dark cave.

"Clancy!" Leigh shouted. The dog darted out of the little hole. He was dusty and his nose was crusted with mud.

"Look at this." Phil bent down and touched a small green shoot. Leigh walked over and looked at what he was holding between his fingers.

It was a white flower. Exactly like the ones she had found in the diary and the closet.

"And then the plumber said, no, I always charge triple." Leigh giggled as she delivered the punch line. Phillip had never noticed what a quirky sense of humor she possessed. He loved the way the skin around her eyes crinkled and the way a little dimple appeared when she smiled. She was beautiful, warm, and intelligent, and everything he wanted in a wife and lifelong companion.

He was about to tell her all that when the sound of sirens ripped through the quiet dining room. Several of the men stood up, their hands on beeping pagers. They rushed from the restaurant, evidently part of the volunteer fire department that served Tear Lake. An orange glow lit up the western end of town through the big picture window.

"Oh, Phil, what should we do?" Chills of alarm crawled up Leigh's arms. She felt the comforting touch of Phil's hand as he took hold of her fingers.

When they looked up Brian was coming up the walk toward the restaurant. His face was smudged with ashes and a deep frown creased his brow. He spoke briefly to the manager.

"I'm sorry to interrupt your dinner, but we have a problem. There was a fire on Seventh Street. Both the Brown and the Johnson homes have been severely damaged, but thankfully nobody was hurt. However, those families have been housing some of our summer program kids. We need volunteers to take the children for the rest of the season."

"How many are there?" a man asked.

"Six boys." Brian's frown deepened when a murmur went through the dining room.

"We would, Brian, but we already have two girls at our house."

"Same with us," another couple agreed. Then one by one it went through the room. Most everyone there was already housing some of the summer kids.

"I'll do it." Leigh stood up to wave at Brian. "I've got tons of room in Gran's old house." Her smile nearly took Phil's breath away. She was so generous and loving. He was happy to think that old house would be filled with the laughter of children and that Leigh wouldn't be alone there. He had been worried about her spending so much time by herself.

"Leigh, I appreciate the offer, but Colorado law requires two adults to supervise these kids. I can't let you take them. I guess I've no choice but to call the city and have those six taken back early."

Leigh's expression cut a wide swath through Phil's heart. She slumped in her chair. Tears welled in her eyes, but she blinked them back and raised her chin a notch. She was so brave.

"I could come and stay at the house, in one of the spare rooms, of course." He regretted his words the minute they were out. It was too soon; her pain was still raw.

Leigh wanted those kids to have their full six weeks. It was such a small amount of time to know happiness and fun. She nodded at Phil. He reached across the table to squeeze her hand.

Leigh thought about having Phil around all the time. She wasn't 100 percent sure this was the best idea, but she was determined to help the kids.

"Let's do it. Phil and I will supervise the kids, Brian."

The crease between his brows eased. "Fine, I'll pick them up and bring them over. How much time do you need to be ready?"

"Practically none at all." Leigh gifted Phil with one of her smiles and he felt blessed beyond words.

Within the hour six boys were snug in Gran's house. Light snow was falling outside.

"Okay, you guys settle down and I'll make some popcorn. Do you want to watch a video?" Phil was sorting through the small box of movies Brian had brought. "I'm glad Brian thought of this, it has been years since we had a child in the house."

"I think I still have some of Cassie's games in the upstairs closet." She ran up the stairs to check. While she was gone Phil used the microwave to make a huge bowl of popcorn. The kids were sprawled on blankets and cushions in front of the television set. Clancy had flopped in the middle of them, eating any popcorn that fell within his reach.

"Can you believe that lazy hound?" Leigh found Operation, Monopoly and Clue. She set them on the dining table.

"He knows when he has it good. The kids love him."

"So do I. Thanks for giving him to me." Leigh leaned up to place a kiss on Phil's cheek. If she hadn't known him so well she might have missed the momentary widening of his eyes.

"When did you know I was the one who left him on the porch?"

"I didn't for sure — until now, that is."

"You tricked me? There are sides to you I've never seen before, Leigh."

"True. And there are sides to you I didn't know either. Thanks for staying here — for the kids. I'm glad you're here for them." He nodded but inside he felt a tiny flare of hope that perhaps she was happy he was here for herself as well.

*November 1, 1859*

Papa says supplies will be brought in once a month. He explained that the wagons are fitted with spikes on the wheels and that the teamsters throw a great hook ahead of them and then with a rope they use a come-along to help the horses pull the wagon forward. The blacksmith makes special shoes for the horses, I'm glad. The poor things work so hard in the cold. It sounds so treacherous. I guess

I'm happy to be snug and warm in our house. I'm knitting Rafael a scarf for Christmas. I miss Rafael so much I can't hardly eat or sleep.

*November 5, 1859*

I saw Rafael today! We went to church and there he was. His poor hands are all red and chapped. I managed to sneak back to the house and found some of Mama's bag balm for Bessie, our milk-cow. Then when I shook Rafael's hand I pressed the little packet into his palm. I hope he realizes what it is for. I can't hardly wait for next Sunday.

# Ten

The next morning Leigh and Phil were a few minutes late. Brian smiled at them as they wrangled their small group of kids to the meeting place where they mingled with the others. Leigh was thankful he had the good grace not to comment on their slightly rumpled appearance — one of the boys had a nightmare and Phil and Leigh didn't get much sleep. In fact she was thinking about going to bed when the sun crept over the eastern horizon. This was definitely not one of her finer moments, and unless she got some coffee she wasn't sure she could stay awake.

Brian nodded toward the pup. "I see you've decided to curtail Clancy's roaming."

Clancy tried to remove the leash that restrained him by a series of cunning acrobatics that kept the children entertained. He finally quit yelping and was now sitting on his fat little behind, pulling to see if the collar would slip off his head.

"That dog is too smart for his own good," Phil commented dryly.

"Yep, whenever Leigh finds out who gave him to her she ought to make him — or her — pay for obedience lessons," Brian suggested with a smile and a wink at Phil.

"The cat, or in this case the Chessie, is out of the bag so you can quit pretending, Brian." Leigh pulled a face.

"Please, don't give her any ideas about that dog. What is our activity for today?" Phil neatly changed the subject.

"Today we take a packed lunch and won't meet until time for the volunteers to pick up the children. We need to let the kids gather whatever they wish for a craft project. Stones, flowers, leaves all make great additions to a nature page each child does, then we insert a photo of them. They are displayed all through the Founders' and Newcomers' Day Festival and the kids take them home as a remembrance of their time here."

"Sounds like fun," Phil said. "Hey, Leigh, do you want to team up? We can take both our groups."

"Sure, why don't we walk around the lake, then up Haunted Trail and down the other side?"

"Clancy doesn't look too enthused at the prospect." Brian pointed at Clancy.

Now the pup had flung himself onto his back. He was eyeballing Tim while the boy rubbed his fat, round belly.

"Poor Clancy," Tim said. "He is sad." Chubby little hands comforted the dour canine. Clancy moaned and Leigh was sure it was in delight, not agony.

"He is spoiled. Tim, if you will help me today, maybe we can teach this brat to walk properly on a leash."

"I'll help." Tim took the leash from Leigh's hand and tugged Clancy to his feet. "C'mon, Clancy. Walk."

And to everyone's surprise, he did.

The sunshine was warm and gentle and had melted away the dusting of snow in the foothills. Exploration was the word of the day while the kids gathered shiny stones, feathers, bits of moss and pinecones. Their backpacks bulged with natural treasures as each child looked for something special to make their page unique and remind them of their favorite activity or place on the mountain. Leigh and Phil walked behind the group, close enough to keep them safe and far enough away to give them space to run, jump and develop their own sense of self. It was a magical time and that magic wrapped invisible threads around Leigh and Phil.

She was falling in love with her husband all over again.

"Clancy, stop!" Tim braced his heels and hung on while the pup tugged and pulled. Tim had found many flowers and blooms for his page, and his backpack was bulging with other lovely bits of bark, sticks and anything that caught his eye.

"Here, buddy, let me help you." Phil took the backpack and passed Clancy's leash over to Leigh. Just as she grabbed him her cell phone started to ring. The "Charge of the Valkyries" echoed through the canyon.

"Now do you see why I hate those things? You can't get away from them. There is no peace with technology. And what is up with that ring?" Phil laughed.

"Women in charge," Leigh replied as she flipped the phone open and walked away from Phil and the kids. She sat down on a fallen log some distance away. "Hello?"

"Hey, sis? Where the heck are you? I've been trying to call you for two days," Tom's deep voice inquired.

"Oops, I guess I forgot to check my message machine. Is everything all right?"

"Sure, I was just concerned. Are you okay?"

"I'm fine. Really."

"I talked to Viv. She tells me you and Phillip are working things out."

"I think we're on the right path, Tom. I won't say things are the way I thought they were, but we're growing closer. He has changed, Tom, and for the better. I still can't get through a day without thinking about how he hurt me, but it doesn't hurt like it once did."

"I'm glad for you, kid. I've come to believe that if there is any love left, any at all, and two people can work it out, they should give it one hundred and ten percent."

"I think we are." Leigh didn't like the sadness in her older brother's voice. "Tom, please say you will come for a visit. We're gearing up for the Founders' and Newcomers' Festival. There is a ton of room even with the kids —"

"Kids? What kids? Is Cassie home from England? Did she bring a friend?"

"No, Cass is still enjoying Europe too much to come home. I'm hosting some of the inner-city kids. Phil is helping me."

"You mean he is staying in the house now?" There was a tone of alarm in the question.

"He is bunking with the children. My room is strictly off-limits. We have a long way to go before that can change."

"I'll be thinking good thoughts for you, kiddo. Now take care."

"I'll do that, and please, Tom, think about my invitation."

"Sure, a houseful of kids and Phillip who needs to have his butt kicked. Great company."

"I know you don't mean that."

"Bye, kid, I love you."

"Bye." Leigh flipped the phone closed and looked at Phil. He was playing with the children, some silly variation of keep away, involving his baseball cap and Clancy. She loved him, but as she had said to Tom, she was protecting her heart.

"My feet hurt," Leigh said.

Phillip grinned at his wife. She was charmingly tousled. Her soft brown hair was windblown, her face was aglow, especially the new freckles across her nose. She had her feet up on the worn brown leather hassock.

"Let me pamper you. Tell you what, the kids and I'll set up the barbeque while you rest. Would you like a glass of iced tea?"

She looked up at him from under the

fringe of her bangs. In all their years of marriage it had been Leigh who did the pampering and Phil who enjoyed being pampered. Maybe it was time to turn the tables.

"No, but I would love a cup of hot herbal tea."

"Coming up. Just let me get the kids started." Phil opened the back door and gave a few gentle orders. Then he set about to make Leigh's tea. It was fascinating for her to lounge in Gran's overstuffed chair and watch him through the doorway. He started humming while he found the mugs and teabags, and set the kettle on the old cooker. Leigh recognized the tune. It was one of the love songs from the Josh Groban CD.

"Coming right up," Phil promised from the other room.

She sighed and snuggled into the comfy upholstery. Then she picked up the journal and started to read.

*November 7, 1859*

I'm getting a new dress! Mama bought an entire ell of dark green wool so she will have a new one too. Papa and some of the men have decided the town should have a winter festival. I think they are doing it because the weather has been so harsh. But at least for one night we will all feast and enjoy ourselves. Papa and some of the other men have gone hunting. So far they have three turkeys and a deer hanging in the icehouse. I love venison stew! Mama says she will make her wonderful gingerbread. I'll get to see Rafael!

*November 11, 1859*

We managed to meet when I pretended to go to the privy last night. I'm so red-faced about that but it was worth it. Rafael is making a special gift for the town. He says it will be ready soon but he won't let me know what it is. He held my hand and even though we were both wearing warm mittens it was wonderful. I put my mitten beneath my pillow tonight and I pray I'll dream of him.

Sunday morning dawned gray and windy. Shivering, Leigh threw a handful of kindling and a log on the hearth and crumpled paper beneath it. She struck a match but a gust of wind swept down the chimney and extinguished it.

"Here let me do that." Phil was beside her.

She had tiptoed past his and the boys' rooms, hoping she wouldn't wake them.

"I didn't mean to wake you." She rubbed her hands together and moved a bit nearer to the hearth when the paper caught the kindling.

"I was already awake. I'm excited about today." Phil smiled at her. It was boyish and charming. Her heart did a little trip inside her chest.

"You know, this is my first baptism," she said.

"Mine too." He used the poker to reposition the log so flames licked across it.

"How do you feel?"

"About the baptism?"

"Uh-hm." She held her hands out toward the fire. The room was beginning to warm. It would be cozy by the time the boys woke up.

"I feel new, Leigh. I guess that is kind of clichéd, but when I was saved I felt God's grace. I know I'm forgiven of my sins. I know I'll go to heaven."

"It must be wonderful," she said softly. "I've been reading the Bible at night and I've some questions I want to ask the pastor. You do seem to be sort of, I don't know, peaceful."

"I am. There is only one thing that could make it better." Phil took a deep breath as if he was going to say more but Leigh wasn't ready for that.

"I'm going to put on some cocoa and toast. Those boys will be up before we know it."

Leigh had tears in her eyes when Phillip rose up from the water of the baptismal. It was a profound and moving experience, and she felt a strange hunger within her. After the service was over she made an appointment to meet with Pastor Miller. She had questions to ask and she hoped he had the answers.

Phil had taken the boys to one of the volunteer families who had organized a picnic to celebrate the collective birthdays of some of the children who would soon be returning to the city. That left Leigh free to do her own thing for the rest of the day.

She headed straight for the old church records at Gran's house. The old pages were yellowed and woefully mixed up. She spread them on the braided rug in the living room and started putting them in order. She had four stacks and a huge pile left to do when she heard the kitchen door open.

"Phil?"

"Actually, you should think of me as the pizza delivery man." He walked through the door with two pizza boxes and a drink tray.

He was grinning from ear to ear. Leigh's heart missed a beat.

They were on such dangerous ground.

She loved him.

She was married to him.

And yet she hadn't got over his betrayal, and though she wished it was otherwise, she had not completely forgiven him and wasn't sure how she could ever do that. It seemed impossible to give up all the pain and hurt.

In spite of all that, she thought him handsome, charming and hard to ignore.

Maybe she shouldn't, she thought. Maybe she shouldn't ignore him, but let him court her, woo her and win her all over again. Perhaps she would learn to trust him more, and leave the hurtful past behind, if she witnessed him go through the entire courtship ritual again.

It was a thought that appealed to her on many levels.

"I knew you would be working on something so I thought I would do dinner. What do you think of my cooking so far?" he teased.

"Smells good." She pulled her legs up under her and sat meditation-style. "I'm hungry."

"Good. I wanted to do something special for you." He gazed into her eyes with such intensity she felt her temperature rise a bit.

Was she blushing?

"Thanks, I appreciate that. In fact, after we eat, maybe you could help me with the church records?" She gave him her most winning smile; at least she hoped it was. It had been a long time since Leigh had flirted.

Phil blinked in surprise. If he didn't know any better he would swear that Leigh was flirting with him. Just the notion made his temperature spike. And being a red-blooded man who was in love with his wife, it was all the encouragement he needed. He stretched out on the floor and flipped open the pizza box.

"Pepperoni or cheese? I did half each."

"Veggie?"

"Coming right up." Phil opened the second box. The aroma of yeasty crust filled his nostrils. He picked up two slices and put them on the oversize napkins furnished by the Pizza Palace.

"Thanks." Leigh took a bite and the flavor of cheese, mushrooms and olives exploded in her mouth. "This is really good."

"I aim to please. Now tell me where you're at with all this." Phil nodded at the stacks of papers.

"Well, so far I'm just separating it by year. It appears that everything starts in 1859."

"Wasn't that the year Tear Lake was founded?"

"Right, but then I don't find much of anything for 1860 and it picks up again in 1861."

Phil picked up a tattered sheet that had come loose from the old bindings. "Hey, this is signed by a Gus Reynolds. Isn't that your Gran's maiden name?"

Leigh looked at the page. "You're right. I need to call Viv. Maybe she can point me in the right direction." She hopped up and headed for the phone.

Phil watched Leigh with a lump in his throat. She was so excited, her cheeks wore two spots of color. Whenever she and Viv got to talking, she ran her hands through her hair and gestured wildly. It was great to watch her. She was so alive, so pretty. He leaned back on his elbows and listened to the conversation, enjoying the sight of her.

"Yes, Viv, a Gus Reynolds. Let me see . . . the date is 1859 — it is smudged but it looks like August."

Leigh was silent, evidently listening to Viv. Then she grabbed the pad by the phone and started scribbling notes.

"Okay, I got it. Uh-huh, right. Fine, call me as soon as you have something." She hung up the phone and grinned at Phil.

"Was she any help?"

"Viv is checking into details. She thinks Gus is buried in the Tear Lake cemetery."

"What are we waiting for? Let's go look."

The afternoon was spent looking at markers in the graveyard but once again the search yielded little. There was a marker that said Reynolds, but it was a family marker so there were no dates or details.

"Sorry we didn't find more." Phil knew she was disappointed.

"Honestly, I wasn't expecting much." She brushed the dust from her knees and stood up but her balance was off and she sort of stumbled — right into Phil's arms. He held her there for half a minute before he kissed her.

It was like being eighteen again, Leigh thought. Phil's arms were strong and steady and her heart tripped a bit. She melted into his embrace. It was a wonderful feeling, her heart soaring, while the man she had married twenty years ago kissed her like they were both teenagers. When he broke the kiss and stared into her eyes it was wonderful. There was such love in them. Love and hope.

He slipped his hand into hers and side by side they walked home to Gran's house.

When they were inside Phil put both hands on Leigh's shoulders and propelled her gently toward the easy chair.

"You sit and read the journal aloud while I straighten out these piles."

Leigh didn't argue. She appreciated Phil backing off and giving her time. She tucked her legs up under her and opened the little book and began to read.

*November 20, 1859*

Excitement has come to Tear Lake. An outlaw gang has been robbing banks, and a man came through town with a warning that they may be headed our way. Papa and the townsmen held a public meeting in the church. The more they spoke, the more frightened Mama became. And though I didn't tell her, I feel the same way. I wasn't supposed to hear but I heard a man tell Papa that a woman and her daughter were robbed and then raped. I asked Mama about it later and she told me what it meant. My face burned with shame and humiliation but I held my tears. Those poor women. An armed guard will be posted at the road coming into Tear Lake. The men will take turns. I was so proud — Rafael was the first to volunteer.

*November 26, 1859*

Tear Lake is no longer the town I've grown to love. Everyone is frightened and jumpy. Nobody laughs or smiles. Neighbors don't visit anymore. Only the men who keep watch speak in groups. I wish spring would come. I pray those outlaws will be caught.

*November 27, 1859*

We woke to a howling blizzard. More than a foot of snow has fallen and it is much deeper in the drifts. Thank the Lord that the men were smart enough to build a great barn near the base of the mountain. All the horses and milk cows are being moved but it is a slow process as each man uses a rope strung along the path to find his way. Poor Papa! His moustache froze to his beard and he had to warm it in order to open his mouth. I hate this weather, but some are saying that at least it will keep the outlaws at bay. I miss Rafael.

# ELEVEN

"Spread the petals out, Tim." Leigh was supervising the position of Tim's dried flower collection for the memory page. Her bright-eyed charges were gathered around her. Some of the kids were sorting pinecones and sticks. Others had gathered rocks and were dividing them according to shape and size. The heavy construction paper and pretty stickers would be attached first and then each child would fashion his page to his liking.

She watched each child and her heart swelled with pride. Each one had grown in confidence. Only a few short weeks ago a frown might have marred a little face; now there was peace. Where formerly a child's lips had turned down in unhappiness, now they grinned and laughed. It was a worthy pursuit to change a child's life, if even for only a few weeks. Leigh felt a surge of pride for the part she had played. She thanked

God for the privilege.

When she thought back to the moment in time when she nearly refused to participate because Phil had shown up, she felt petty and small-minded. How foolish she had been to even consider putting her own needs above these children. And in the end Phil himself had turned out to be their champion. The money from the sale of his sports car would make a difference. Brian told her all the craftsmen, laborers and construction workers in town had volunteered their services. The only cost was going to be the materials, and a large portion of those would be greatly discounted. It was like Habitat for Humanity, in a way. The men and women of Tear Lake would put their sweat equity into the future of each and every child that would ever come to Tear Lake for a summer of laughter, fun and learning.

"A penny for your thoughts?" Phil's shadow fell over the page Leigh was working on. She had decided to do one for herself to remember this extraordinary summer.

"I was just thinking how much fun I've had with these kids. And how much difference six weeks has made in their young lives."

"It has been great. I've felt as if God was giving me a second chance. I realize how much better I could've done with Cassie. She is wonderful, but that is thanks to you, Leigh. These kids, the boys especially, have been terrific. I've loved fishing, hiking and roughhousing with them all. This summer has been incredible in lots of ways."

She smiled at Phil. His words warmed her like the summer sun. It was a strange paradox the way the journal was written during the harsh cold of winter while she was enjoying the halcyon days of summer. In just two days the children would be going home.

Leigh wasn't sure what that would mean for her and Phillip.

Would he stay on at Gran's house? There were so many things that were still unsettled, unspoken. Was he planning on staying in Tear Lake? Was she? Their house in the city was paid for and would be easy to sell — if. But that was a big if when she wasn't even clear yet about whether or not they had a solid future together. Leigh was sure of only one thing: she wasn't willing to settle for the kind of marriage she'd had with Phil before. If they reconciled, it was going to have to be with a whole new direction and understanding between them.

It was going to be a marriage with God in it.

And if she did stay in Tear Lake, she would have to find a house of her own because Gran's house was owned by the whole family and not available for just one. In fact, the more she thought about it, the more she thought she should start checking the paper and looking for something.

"There you go again. Off in another world," Phil said.

"Oh, I guess I was. I was thinking I need to start looking for a house."

"A house?" Phil's stomach had just dropped to his feet. He thought — he had presumed. Maybe his hopes for a future were unfounded. "Why do you need a house?"

"Because I think I may stay in Tear Lake, and if I do I can't camp out at Gran's. It belongs to all of us for summer visits and getaways. She never intended for any one of us to just move in and stay."

Phil's heart was being squeezed by an iron fist. Leigh's words stunned him. Until this moment he hadn't thought beyond earning her forgiveness. But now he realized there was a lot beyond that. Of course she wouldn't want to return to the house where she had experienced so much pain at his hands. She probably hated their house, hated the city.

They needed a fresh start. But he wanted to do this right.

If they sold the house and they both stayed here, she might think he was doing it because it was easier than facing what had happened; then it would only be a patch on something still broken.

If he broached the subject and bungled it, then Leigh might be out of his life forever. *But do I have the courage to risk losing her?* He turned the question over in his mind and his heart while Leigh settled herself and read aloud from the journal.

*December 1, 1859*

We had our wonderful festival of ice last night — that was what he called it. And he asked me to call him Rafe and I tingled from my head to my toes when he called me Carrie. Nobody but him has ever called me that. It is wonderful, our own little secret, and I shall never tell another soul. We had one dance together. Papa said it would be unseemly to have more than a single dance with any one young man, so I had to dance with anyone who asked. Homer Griggs is a nice boy, but he stepped on my foot and then his face turned so red

I thought he might burst into flames. The food was wonderful but the best part of the night was when I managed to step outside for a breath of air and Rafe handed me a little paper wrapped object. I wasn't able to open it until I got home. It is a piece of blue-grey glass in the shape of a tear. That is what his skill is; he is a glass blower and can make wondrous things. It has a tiny hole in it and I put it on a slender ribbon. I'll wear it forever.

*December 24, 1859*

It is Christmas Eve. I haven't been able to write because Mama has been so sick. She went to nurse a family that had become ill and when she returned home she was shaking, but she was hot as coals. Papa is praying over her right now. Please, God, spare my mama.

*January 3, 1860*

Winter has been so long. I wonder how long it will go on. Christmas was spare and cold. Mama is still very weak, and is able to only take broth. Papa says I've grown up this winter and I'm becoming a young woman. I do feel different. Seeing my mama so ill and knowing how close she came to death changed something inside me. I still miss Rafe, but it is a different kind of longing I feel now. When will spring come to the mountains?

*January 23, 1860*

The sun has been shining all day and I find my spirits lifted. Mama was able to sit in a chair out in the sun. Papa insisted she stay wrapped in Granny's old quilt but I think some color has returned to her cheeks. Snow is still thick on the northern side of anything in town, but I see a hint of spring. Rafe was waiting for me beside the blacksmith's today. He asked me if he could court me! I thought my knees would buckle and I would fall right at his feet. It is a little forward but he doesn't know about American customs so I forgive him. Besides, he explained it wouldn't be too smart to talk to my papa first and then find out I wasn't interested. If only he knew how much I've waited for this day.

"It is a romantic story, isn't it?" Phil said while Leigh was blinking back tears in her eyes.

"Yes, I hope it all worked out for her." She closed the journal and rubbed her hands over the letters on the front. "I just wish we could find out who she was."

"Well, we have a great clue now that we know her name."

"Carrie . . . Carrie with the last name that begins with T," Leigh mused aloud. "And the piece of glass on a ribbon."

"You don't think it survived, do you?" Phil's voice held doubt.

"I don't know. There is something about that glass teardrop, something that seems familiar." Leigh frowned and tried to dredge up the whisper of recognition but whatever it was, if indeed it was anything, was buried deep. "I can't remember. Maybe it will come to me."

"In the meantime, why don't you call Viv?" Phil grinned.

"Good idea."

Leigh picked up the phone and hit speed dial. Vivian answered on the third ring.

"Hello."

"Hey, Viv."

"I knew it would be you. I found some records on microfiche at the LDS church."

"Tell me what you have." Leigh was excited.

"There was a Gus Reynolds. He had a daughter named Carolina Rachel and a son. In fact his son is our great-great-grandfather Thomas."

"You're kidding?"

"Nope. Does this help?"

"Yes, it does. So our great-great-grandfather had a sister? Why didn't we know about this?"

"It looks like she died young. There was a big age difference between her and Thomas."

"Thanks, Viv —"

"Oh, no, you don't. You're not going to thank me and hang up. You're not getting off this phone until you tell me what is going on with you and Phil."

Leigh took a deep breath. How could she sum up the change? How could she explain?

"Have you been able to forgive him?" Vivian asked.

"I — I don't know." Leigh glanced around to make sure Phil was in the living room and unable to hear everything she said. "No, I guess I haven't. Not completely."

"It's tough, isn't it? When I'm faced with a problem like this, I pray," Viv said softly.

"You? You pray? But your life is so perfect and so, so . . . peaceful."

Vivian laughed. "Don't sound so shocked. Did you think your older spinster sister was somehow immune to God? Or did you think since I was alone, I don't have family problems so I don't need the Lord? I know over the last few years we haven't spent much time together. Living in different towns — your family schedule — but I should've told you that I started attending church and was saved. It has changed my life."

Leigh was surprised, but it made sense. Vivian had sounded different. She was warmer, more loving — not that she hadn't been a great sister, she had, but there was another layer to her and a depth that hadn't been there before.

First Phillip and now Vivian.

Was Leigh missing out?

"Hey, say something," Viv said. "I didn't know my revelation was going to shock you into silence."

"No, it isn't that. It is just — I can't put it into words."

"Don't feel like you have to. But I do want to say one thing, Leigh. In the Lord's Prayer we ask to be forgiven as we forgive others. I've always found those words particularly compelling. I mean if I'm going to be given forgiveness and walk in God's grace in direct proportion to how much I forgive, I find myself striving even harder not to judge. My motives are not the purest, but it helps me put things in perspective. Now I'm going to hang up. I'll keep looking into your mystery of the initials. You go have a talk with God."

Leigh didn't have much time to have a conversation with the Lord, because it was time for the children to put the finishing touches on their memory pages. Her front porch had been turned into an artsy production area. Hot glue, construction paper, stickers, ribbon, wood and paint littered the wide floorboards.

"Need help," Tim said, holding up one of his pressed, dried flowers. He had a wonderful variety of blooms, including the still-unidentified white flower he had found.

"Okay, you get ready and I'll put the glue on. Okay?" Leigh picked up the hot glue gun and squeezed the trigger. A hot, clear blob appeared. She touched it to Tim's background and then when she nodded he stuck the bloom in place.

"Flowers are pretty." He gave her a gap-toothed grin. He had lost a tooth and been thrilled to find the tooth fairy had left him a coin in exchange.

On the other end of the porch Phil was carefully using a knife to cut some twigs into a manageable length. Leigh paused a moment to watch him. She thought about Vivian's words. At the end of the day, did mercy and forgiveness depend on how much we had given out ourselves? Leigh wasn't sure. She made a mental note to talk to Pastor Miller about it when she went to the church later. As soon as she helped the kids finish their pages, she had an appointment to meet Brian and fit the last bits of the window together. Today she would finally see the entire scene.

Even though Brian had suggested she find a partner to help her restore the window, she had declined. It had taken more time, but she had done it all by herself with Brian's tutelage. Now the window would be revealed.

"Hey, buddy, how is it going?" Phil had left his group doing the final part of their pages. Each boy was bent in concentration. He ruffled Tim's hair and plopped down in a nearby wicker chair.

"Flowers are pretty," Tim told Phil, pointing to the arrangement he had made. By tomorrow each child would have a finished page to display and then take home.

"I'm going to miss these kids." Phil's words brought Leigh's head up with a snap. She would never have expected it from him. But the emotion in his voice was undeniable.

"It has been nice to have them here."

Phil wondered if Leigh felt the same about him but he certainly wasn't going to ask. It was eating him alive, but he was keeping his mouth shut. Rash, impulsive behavior had broken her heart and driven her away; he wasn't going to make a similar mistake again.

"When are you going to tell me what your surprise is?" Phil asked. Leigh had been plotting and planning with Brian and Pastor Miller about something — some present — but she wouldn't share any details with Phil. A part of him was wounded, but the bigger part knew he deserved it. Why should Leigh want to share secrets with a man who had hurt her? He knew her heart might never heal, but he was praying it would. He also knew if it took an eternity for her to trust him, he was willing to wait — he would wait — and endure because that was the right course of action. It was just, and it was fair that he be willing to risk his heart, his time, and his future for Leigh.

And if she did forgive him, he would fall down on his knees and thank God for it.

"Here, let me sweep up while you read more from the journal." Phil took the broom from Leigh and began to clear away the rubbish left from the kids' creations. There were bits of string, grass, twigs, stones, paper, sticks, stems and even a live lizard that had been liberated before it was sacrificed to art. Now it sat sunning itself, either too stunned or too comfortable to move.

"Suits me. I wonder if the historical society would have any information on the Stockton gang?"

"I dunno, want me to check with them?" Phil offered.

"Would you?"

"I'd love to play detective for you." Phil longed for the days when Leigh came to him with requests. He had been such a fool. A blind, self-indulgent idiot.

"Sure, that would be great. Right now I'm tired and I want to see what other clues we can find right here." Leigh ducked into the house and came back out with the little journal. She flopped into the old oak rocker and opened the book where the ribbon bookmark rested. Phil continued sweeping, but she was aware that all his attention was on her voice as she read the next entry in the journal.

*February 7, 1860*

The newest part of Tear Lake where some of the most recent immigrants had been living in tents was hit by spring floods. The sun has started melting the snow on the mountain and now the main street is running like a creek. Our cow had to be moved and Mr. Gruber's draft horses are now in a high, dry meadow that Rafe found. He looked so thin and worn as he stood before the fire warming his hands, I nearly wept for him. But his smile is still a thing of beauty, and my papa shook his hand and thanked him for telling him about the sheltered meadow. I wonder if Rafe is making his fortune and if his beautiful hands will ever be the same. Next Sunday I'm going to speak to him — in front of Papa. I'm not ashamed of him, and it is time that Papa realized I'm not a little girl anymore.

*February 16, 1860*

I'm furious! I saw Rafe in the feed and grain and so I stopped to talk to him. He handed me a flower that was different than anything I had seen before. Papa came in and saw us. His face was like a thundercloud. He ordered me home saying Mama needed me. And though my mama is still weak she wasn't in any danger. At supper Papa told me I needed to find a suitable friend. Suitable? What does he mean? My father has always said we're brothers and sisters in Christ — what could be more suitable than to care about a good Christian man? I want to talk to him more about it but right now Mama is feeling poorly again and I must see to the chores. Bessie needs milking and I must make bread for the week.

# TWELVE

Founders' Day was picture perfect. The sun was shining, the light breeze kept the midges away and made the lovely, bright, multicolored streamers and flags flutter in a most charming way. Everyone in town had turned out. Many visitors walked the quaint streets. There were craft booths, funnel cake stalls and roasted turkey legs for sale, as well as the usual merchants moving their wares out to the old cobbled street and dressing in period clothing. Ladies in full skirts with parasols mingled with men in spats, suspenders and shirt garters.

"You look great," Phil told Leigh as he adjusted his own stiff collar. They had found the clothes in a trunk in Gran's attic and had decided to come in costume.

"Thanks." Leigh plucked at the muttonchop-shaped sleeve and held herself more erect. Funny how these clothes made her feel more feminine and prettier than jeans and a sweatshirt ever could. She saw Brian in the crowd. He waved and maneuvered through the clutch of people.

"Hey, Brian. Did you get the children dropped off at the church?" Leigh asked. It had been a bittersweet joy to get the children ready today. After the parade and the mayor's speech, the kids would be leaving for the year.

"Yep, the youth group volunteers have got them busy tying ribbons on the trees around the church. We want it to look pretty when you make your presentation, Leigh." He had his hair parted in the middle and slicked down with gel.

"Presentation? I thought I was just going to give it to Pastor Miller." The thought of getting up and speaking in front of a crowd brought a tight fist of fear to her stomach. She had never been very good at speaking to strangers and the town was full of them.

"Sorry, but the pastor decided it was such a great gift that he wanted everyone to know the details." Brian grinned. "We never knew about it until you came along, Leigh. The town is grateful."

Phil touched Leigh's shoulder and the gesture eased her nerves. "Okay, I'll do my best."

"I've faith in you. I better get going, Shirley and I are hosting a booth for the historical society. See you after the parade."

"Hey, I want to come over later and ask you some questions about some outlaws who evidently worked this area about one hundred years ago."

Brian's eyes lit up. "Shirley would love that. She is a wealth of information and is always saying she would love a research job. You will make her day."

"Terrific, then I'll see you later." Phil turned to see a frown on Leigh's face. "What?"

She heaved a sigh. "The presentation. This wasn't exactly what I had in mind."

"What can I do to help?"

She stared at Phil for a full minute before she spoke. "All right, you can help me."

"I'll do anything."

"Let me rehearse. I'll use you as my audience and give a short speech."

"Does this mean I get to find out what the gift is?"

"No. This is pretend, remember?" She laughed and slipped her hand into the crook of Phil's arm. Then she pulled him toward an empty bench where she pushed on his shoulder until he sat down. Then, like a nervous teenager, she cleared her throat, rubbed her palms on the old-fashioned shirtwaist and began to speak.

His heart filled with love and admiration. He hung on her every word and his curiosity about her gift to the town kicked up another notch. The period dress complimented her small waist and long, graceful neck. She clasped her slender fingers together and white-knuckled her fear into submission.

A half-hour later Leigh had shooed Phil away so she could meet with Pastor Miller at the church. The parade was due to start in forty-five minutes. That gave Phil enough time to visit the booth where Brian's fiancée Shirley was working. He had never met her, but felt like they were old friends because Brian talked about her frequently, and of course they saw her briefly each day when she helped with the kids.

She had long brown hair and a petite build. When Brian introduced her, two deep dimples appeared in her cheeks. Shirley and Brian made a great couple.

"I'm so pleased to see you. Bri said you were coming to see me. Something about an outlaw gang?"

Phil grinned. Her happy, outgoing attitude was infectious. No wonder Brian was always in such a good mood. Nobody could spend very long with Shirley without smiling. Phillip hoped Brian wouldn't make the same mistakes he had. Sometimes the most precious treasure was right in front of a guy's face.

"Yes, Leigh has found an old journal in her grandmother's attic. It makes reference to the Stockton gang. Have you ever heard of them?"

"Yes, I have. The Stockton gang was very successful — if you consider robbery, rape and murder a success. They terrorized the mining camps on Red Mountain and raided ranches over the border into New Mexico. They met a bad end, but for several years they pretty much did what they wanted."

"No law?"

"Not a lot at that time. Townspeople banded together and did what they could, but times were different. A lot of towns went years before they hired a sheriff. The law could be a hundred miles or more away. It wasn't like you could lock your valuables in a vault. The assay office in most towns had a small safe or strongbox, but that could easily be taken if the robber was determined. Nobody knows how much gold and silver they made off with, but it was surely a considerable amount. Of course Tear Lake had their own villain."

"What do you mean?"

"Evidently, and this is mostly oral history, you understand, at about the same time the Stocktons were raiding in Colorado and the New Mexico Territory, there was a man who made off with all Tear Lake's ore that was awaiting transport off the mountain. The story is that he was a 'wolf in the fold.' Trask was the name, I think, but I don't know too much about it. My grandfather had heard the story from his grandmother. There are a couple of different versions. One thing everyone seems to agree about is that the man and the 'Tear Lake treasure' disappeared and were never seen again."

The parade was long, loud and colorful. Tear Lake's very own brass band marched ahead of the float with a baton-wielding major at the head. There was even the Coal County Sheriff's posse, decked out in chaps and pale tan Stetsons, mounted on paint horses that pranced up Main Street.

"This is great," Leigh said. Phil only had eyes for her. She was jumping up trying to get a better view of the floats. "Look, it's the kids."

The float was made of chicken wire and bunting. Every inner-city child who had enjoyed the mountain this summer was aboard. They were tanned and happy and tossed candy to the observers as they rolled by. The parade wound its way through town and doubled back.

"That is my cue to head to the church," Leigh said. "Will you be rooting for me?"

"Not only will I be rooting for you, I'll be sitting right up front." Phil placed a tender kiss on her cheek. "Go knock 'em dead, sweetheart."

Leigh's heart was beating like the wings of a captured bird. She told herself it was the prospect of getting up to speak before the crowd, but she knew it was because she still cared for Phil and harbored hope for their future.

If only she could trust and forgive him — completely.

Phil was walking toward the church, eager to find a place at the front so Leigh would see him when she got up to speak. He was curious to see what her gift would be. Maybe she had cashed in a certificate of deposit and was making a cash donation.

No. Leigh was never a person to throw money at a problem. Whatever she decided to give, it would be something more "hands on."

There were so many people gathered outside, the throng was slowing down to a crawl. Phil was almost to the church doors when he felt a heavy hand on his shoulder.

"Phillip." The deep voice halted him.

He turned to look into the stern, weathered face of his brother-in-law. "Hello, Tom."

"I think it is time we had a talk, man to man."

Phil nodded. "Actually, I'm surprised it took you so long."

Leigh looked out over the crowd in the church. There were friends and neighbors and many, many strangers. But there was no sign of Phil. A sharp pang of disappointment shot through her. He'd promised he would be here.

"But he has broken promises before," she whispered to herself. A small sprout of her newfound trust withered and died as she stood near the pulpit and waited for Pastor Miller to introduce her.

Tom and Phil walked around to the back of the church toward the graveyard. The murmur of voices inside the church was a low rumble, and many people were still down on Main Street visiting the booths and enjoying the tranquil beauty of Tear Lake.

"You know, Phil," Tom began without

preamble, "I could take you apart for what you did to my baby sister." He looked at Phil with cold blue eyes.

Phil nodded. What could he say? His guilt was no less powerful than Tom's anger.

"Viv has told me everything. I guess I've a pretty good idea of what you did, so you don't need to fill in the details, but I do have one question. What the hell were you thinking?"

For a moment the silence seemed to choke off any reply that Phil might make. Then he pulled himself together and looked into Tom's furious gaze.

"I wasn't thinking. I was a stupid, spoiled, indulgent fool, Tom. You know, I hope you do beat me to a bloody pulp. God knows I deserve it and more, but the fact is, I don't think you could do anything to make me hurt more than I do each time I look into Leigh's eyes and know I put that pain there."

Tom glared at him and flexed his fists at his sides as if he were fighting the urge to throw a punch. Then his expression changed to bitter resignation and he heaved a deep sigh.

"I'm not going to beat you to a pulp. I should, but I'm not going to do it for two reasons."

"What reasons?" Phil was curious.

"One — my sister loves you — she picked you, so you can't be all bad. And two — I hate hypocrites, and that is what I would be if I judge you, because I ruined my own marriage. Oh, I didn't cheat like you did, but I destroyed the best part of my life." Tom glared at Phil. "Let me give you the wisdom of my fifty years of living, Phil. It takes two to make a marriage, but it only takes one to destroy it. It takes one cruel heart, or one self-centered partner, or one faithless spouse, or one too many hours of neglect in the name of career. A marriage will die like a tender bud on a vine. If you love my sister, and I hope for her sake you do, then you had better grow up, straighten up and do what is right. Because if we ever have this little talk again —"

"Believe me, Tom, I'll never hurt Leigh again —"

"It doesn't matter if I believe you. The person you need to convince is Leigh." Tom spat the words out and then he turned and stalked away.

Phil watched him for only a moment. Then he turned in the opposite direction and hurried to the church doors, all the while praying he wasn't too late to keep his promise to Leigh.

"And so I thought this would make the perfect gift for the town. I've Brian and his patient skill to thank for getting it back to its former glory."

Leigh's sweet voice wafted through the church. Phil hurried in, rudely elbowing his way into the building and up the aisle. He smiled when he saw Leigh standing there in her old-fashioned clothes with a large square of something wrapped in brown paper in her arms.

She looked down the aisle and her gaze met Phil's. A tiny smile curved her lips and something warm and wonderful flashed in her eyes.

It was joy.

"So I now give the town of Tear Lake this lovely bit of history. I will be so pleased to see it here in the church again." Leigh tore through the paper. She held the object up for all to see.

It was a beautiful stained glass window in a new oak frame. In stunning colors of red and gold, a sunrise broke over the outline of a mountain — the mountain that towered over Tear Lake. And below that, in a cleft made of green, brown and grays, was a dark cave and at the mouth of the cave was a scatter of white blooms.

"The same white flower Leigh found in

the old journal," Phil said as the roar of applause and appreciation filled the church.

# THIRTEEN

"No, really, it was my pleasure." Leigh shook another hand and tried to make her way to Phil. She had been so happy to see him there, watching her, supporting her with his presence. She wanted to reach him, touch him, and be with him. The crowd parted and she saw him. Right behind him was her brother Tom.

"You decided to accept my invitation!" She threw herself into his arms and for a moment she was ten years old again. Tommy was the greatest brother in the world. He never teased Leigh, never tried to leave her behind or keep her out of his fun. He had been her hero through junior high and, when in high school he was a top athlete in both football and swimming, she had been part of his cheerleading squad. She had been the matron of honor at his and Rose-mary's wedding. She pulled away and looked at him. There were deep lines around his eyes that had never been there before. And his blue eyes were haunted with the shadows of pain.

"I decided I needed a break. I thought I would drown a few worms, sit on the bank and contemplate life. If you have enough room at Gran's house."

"That house is as much yours and Viv's as it is mine. You know that. Besides, the children are leaving today."

"The children?" Tom frowned.

"We have been hosting some of the inner-city children."

"We?" Tom raised a brow at Phil. "I didn't realize that Phillip had moved into the house."

Leigh flushed a little but she smiled. "Not exactly moved in —"

"State requirements are that two adults need to be in supervision. Leigh let me stay in a guest room. For the kids," Phil was quick to explain. Then he realized how odd their situation was. He was Leigh's husband, but he had forfeited his right to share her bed.

"Of course, for the kids," Tom repeated. Leigh wanted to pull him aside and ask him if he thought she was being stupid, but she couldn't very well do that with Phil standing right there. Suddenly there was a great commotion and the sound of panic in raised voices.

"What is it?" Leigh asked as one of the youth volunteers rushed by. The girl had tears streaming down her face.

"Oh, I'm so sorry. I only took my eyes off him for a minute. I never thought he could move so fast."

"Who? What has happened?" Phillip pulled a hankie from the old-fashioned pocket of his dark frock coat. He always carried a clean handkerchief — Leigh found it a charming eccentricity.

"Little Tim. He has gone missing. The whole town is looking for him."

"Clancy, sit." Leigh had returned to Gran's house with Phil and Tom. She had changed her clothes and brought Clancy in from the backyard. Tom was down on one knee stroking the dog's ears. "This is a fine fella. Where'd you get him, Leigh?"

"He was a present — from Phillip."

Phillip was busy gathering supplies. He had a flashlight and a couple of bottles of water when he emerged from the kitchen.

"A gift from Phillip, huh?"

Tom's face was unreadable, but she knew what was going on behind those still, blue eyes. She knew because she had felt the same way when Rose divorced Tom. Her family was fiercely loyal to one another. She and Viv loved Rose, but Tom was their brother. It had been very difficult for the first year or so to keep from saying something to Rose. She had bitten her tongue more than once, so she knew that Tom was doing it now.

"Ready?" Phil was shoving a length of nylon rope and the other items into a net bag.

"Phil?" Leigh's stomach knotted in fear when she saw those items. This was serious. Tim was wonderfully functional but he was just a little boy. And the mountain could be deadly, especially when the sun set. She said a prayer as they rushed from the house and hurried up the path to the mountain.

A cool breeze blew up. Clancy wasn't moving as fast up the path as he had been. He seemed confused and distracted.

"Do you really think he is smelling anything or is he just climbing up the mountain?" Tom's face was in long shadow since the sun was dropping behind the pinnacles of rock in the west.

"I pray he is tracking Tim, but there is no way to know. He likes Tim, and I think Clancy can smell as well as any dog, but he is just a pup and untrained at that." Leigh was growing more worried the later it got.

"My money is on his nose." Phil had helped Leigh scramble up a scatter of loose stones when Clancy suddenly changed direction and hauled hard on the leash. Her legs were aching and the weight of worry made each step torture.

She glanced back and saw the wink of lights. Another group of townspeople were on the mountain looking for Tim. The other children were gathered at the church. The parents in the city were awaiting the return of their children. They had been notified there would be a delay, but no details had been given. She hoped that Tim would be found and they would only be a little delayed returning home.

Darkness crept like a thief across the mountain, turning paths into obstacle courses and changing picturesque rock formations into death traps. Phil switched on his flashlight. The shaft of light moved around erratically while he tried to keep the beam focused just ahead of Clancy.

"Careful! Rock!" Tom shouted when Phil's foot dislodged a rock. It tumbled by them and pinged its way down the side of the mountain toward the fireflies of light carried by the other group. Leigh could only hope someone below heard the warning.

Clancy stopped to sniff the air. He ran a few paces in one direction and then turned and doubled back. He did that several times while Leigh's heart lodged in her throat. And then with a bark he plunged onward at a faster pace, as if beckoned by some invisible force. There was no path where he scampered, but the humans did their best to keep up. He led them on through the darkness.

Phil moved the light around. And then there was a sound — faint — unintelligible.

"Listen." Leigh stopped walking, tense with the effort of trying to hear. A sound — could it be a whimper? It came again and this time Clancy barked. He kept barking while Tom and Phil came to stand on either side of him. Thcy strained to see into the stygian gloom.

Once more the beam of light slid over the rocks. Once more the faint sound answered.

"Look, there is an opening." Tom moved forward and began to pull at boulders, some of them three times the size of a bowling ball. Then Clancy tore the leash from Leigh's grasp. He slipped past Tom and into a crevice in the rocks.

"Clancy!" Leigh cried out, but it was too

late. She could hear the sound of his barks growing fainter and fainter.

"Oh, no. I hope we haven't lost them both," Tom said.

"Praying is the best thing we can do," Phil agreed.

Leigh bowed her head. With tears running down her face she did pray to God above. The mountain grew quiet.

A sudden flash of light and then a rumble. Raindrops, cold and fat, began to pelt Leigh's head. In moments her hair was wet and dripping into her eyes. She wrapped her arms around herself and hunched against the rain.

"You're not dressed for this, Leigh," Tom said.

She glanced back down the mountain and saw the winking lights. Some of them were retreating, going back down the mountain. She wanted to shout, to tell them to stop.

They couldn't leave — not with Clancy in the crevice — not with Tim missing.

"Don't give up. You can't give up," she murmured. And in that moment, with the cold rain falling on her, Phillip and Tom, she realized she was talking aloud.

Life was sometimes hard. Sometimes it was lonely and hurtful. Sometimes it shoved you down hard, skinned your knees and broke your heart. Happily-ever-after wasn't a guarantee. But Pastor Miller told her God had a guarantee and it was unbreakable. He would always offer His love and salvation. All we had to add was faith.

He was always with her. He never left her, never abandoned her, and no matter what she did, thought, or said, no matter how much of a failure she was, He never gave up.

Never.

Clancy sprang from the cleft with a yelp. He was covered in dirt and cringed as the stinging raindrops hit him. Tom rushed forward and crouched down beside the pup. He tugged on the leash that trailed inside the crevice.

It wouldn't come out.

"I think there is something at the end of this leash," he told Leigh.

"Let me help." Phillip was beside Tom. Slowly, as if they were reeling in a big fish, they pulled steadily on the leash.

"Clancy." Tim's voice was unmistakable. "Clancy, come back."

"It's him." Leigh wanted to help, but there was no room for her. Between Clancy barking encouragement, and Phil and Tom, she couldn't see anything.

The rain began to fall harder and flashes

of blue-white light turned night to day for an instant. Leigh's heart leapt to her throat. Tom and Phil were in an awkward position at the edge of a cliff. The rain was causing little rivulets to stream off the rocks above. One stream was washing away the earth beneath her brother's knees, the other runnel was pouring into the crevice.

"Oh, dear Lord, please don't let Tim drown."

"I'm going to move these rocks," Tom shouted above the din of thunder.

"Careful, one wrong move could bring down the whole thing," Phillip warned.

Tom moved a rock at the same moment Phillip tugged on the leash. Tim emerged like a mole. He was covered in thick mud, his clothes were soaked, but he was hanging onto Clancy's leash for dear life.

"Tim, what were you thinking?" Leigh cleaned mud from his mouth and his eyes.

"Treasure! Clancy find treasure." He choked and sputtered.

Then the earth Tom was standing on shifted. Water undermined the rock. Mud sifted away. Phil shone the flashlight in his direction at the moment Tom went down. There was a horrible clatter of falling rocks and a dull thud.

"Tom!" Leigh screamed.

Her brother had slipped from the muddy ledge when it flaked off.

"Phillip!" Leigh screamed. She ran to the edge and tottered there, nearly going over herself until Phil snatched her back.

"Here, hold this." He shoved the flashlight into her hand and got down on his belly. The rain was falling hard, the little rivulets growing into rushing streams of water. It was crashing over the rocks, making a waterfall that began to hum with the force of the water.

"Tim, you stay right there. Do you hear me? You stay right there with Clancy." Both boy and dog were wet, cold and miscrable. But she could tell by the look in Tim's eyes that he was going to obey.

"Leigh, can you hand me down Clancy's leash?" Phil yelled.

Quick as she could slog through the muck and water, she unsnapped the pup's leash and returned to the edge. Phil took it from her hand and lowered it down.

"Hold on tight, Tom!" he yelled and then he crabbed his way backward. The double-stitched leather was pulled taut. It took long minutes, but finally Tom's wet head appeared at the edge of the cliff.

"Tom, Tom. Oh, thank you, God." Leigh was laughing and crying.

"Go down the mountain. Take the flashlight and Tim. Find Brian and tell him to bring help," Phillip snapped out orders.

"What's wrong?" Leigh's heart skipped a beat as she looked from Phil to Tom, who was now sprawled on the cliff edge. He was wet, shivering, but he made no effort to get up from the mud.

"Tom's ankle is broken."

The rain made the rescue slow, but within two hours Tom was sitting in Gran's overstuffed chair with his cast propped up on the old hassock. He was in dry clothes with a mug of black coffee in his hand. Children were sprawled around his chair. He was the hero of the hour — along with Clancy, who had been bathed and blow-dried to a chocolate mousse with soulful eyes.

Shirley and Brian stood near the fireplace. He had promised the children they would hear the story of Haunted Trail by firelight, and since the rain was still pelting against the windows, Leigh had suggested they use Gran's living room for this final tradition before the children left. The seasoned logs crackled while Phil went through the house switching off lights until only the glow from the hearth remained.

"Now you will learn the story of Haunted

Trail," Brian began. Shirley sat near him on the floor listening in rapt attention though Leigh was sure she must've heard the tale many times. "Long ago, long before your grandparents were smaller than you, Tear Lake was a mining camp. There was gold and silver and men came from all over to dig it out of the mountain. But there were also bad men who wanted to steal the treasure."

Gooseflesh rose on Leigh's arms. She sat up straighter. His choice of words made her pay more attention.

"A man who lived here took the gold and silver, or so the story goes. He disappeared one night and was never seen again."

"What has that got to do with the Haunted Trail?" one boy asked, clearly disappointed by the violence-free story.

Brian grinned. "Maybe nothing. But folks say that he left behind a sweetheart and if the moon is just right and there is no wind, you can hear her calling his name as she roams the mountain in search of him."

A collective murmur went through the crowd.

"Now you heard the story and I see the bus has pulled up. Come on, kids, I have to get you back to your parents. They missed you for six long weeks. And I know you have many stories to share with them."

Leigh picked up the journal while Phillip made cocoa in the kitchen. She missed the boys, but silence had settled over Gran's house and she so wanted to get back to the story. Each night they learned a bit more and she felt they were on the verge of solving the riddle.

"Is that the journal, sis? Viv was telling me about it." Tom shifted himself.

"Are you in pain?"

"No, the doctor gave me something. I'm quite comfortable. Now tell me about the journal."

Tom had never been comfortable being the center of attention. Leigh saw that had not changed a bit.

"It is better if I read it aloud. You haven't missed too much." She opened the little book and began where the ribbon was. The sound of the fire and Clancy's tired sighs seemed far away as she was once more pulled into the story from long ago.

*March 1, 1860*

We finally have our own pastor! Papa has done a fine job, but he is a merchant, not a minister. Now we have our very own. At first we thought he was going to ride circuit and we would have him one Sunday in four but Pastor Johnson has chosen to remain in Tear Lake. He says he hopes men from the surrounding mining camps will come and attend with us. He is such a nice man. Thank you, Lord.

*March 4, 1860*

I met Pastor Johnson coming from the mercantile. He was so kind I found myself pouring out my heart to him right there in the street. He handed me his hankie and I was so embarrassed to find tears were running down my face. It was just everything — the flood victims needing more than anyone has to give, Mama being so poorly and Papa's strange attitude about Rafe. I just broke down. He walked with me to the church and together we prayed. I feel much better now.

*March 8, 1860*

Rafe sent me a message through Pastor Johnson. He has made his fortune! It will not be long before he can speak to my papa about courting me. He wanted to do it right away but I asked him to wait because Mama is still so weak. But it is warmer every day and she is getting some color back in her cheeks. Mrs. Gruber came to visit, but Mama wouldn't see her because she said she didn't want the town gossiping about how awful she looked. I never knew my mama was a vain woman, but she laughed and I saw a flicker of strength in her eyes. Oh, and Rafe kissed me. It was only a light kiss on the cheek, but it was like dynamite exploding inside me. I love him.

*April 1, 1860*

Rafe came after church to speak with Papa and Mama. He was dressed in his very best. His dark hair was slicked back and he was shaved clean as a plucked hen. I was so proud of him. Papa listened to every word and then he told Rafe that I wasn't old enough for a beau. I left the room in tears. How could Papa be so cruel? Marjorie Jones was married last week and she is a full year younger than I. I saw Rafe walking away from our house. He had a little bouquet of those strange flowers. I snuck out the back door and ran to him. I don't care what Papa says. I offered to run off with Rafe, but he said no. He wants us to start our lives the right way. He wants Papa to realize how much we love each other. We held hands and prayed. I know God will answer our prayers.

*May 8, 1860*

The Stockton gang is raiding again. They stole cattle from a ranch in the valley below. The sheriff formed a posse and chased them into the New Mexico Territory. Everyone knows they will be back. The men met to discuss the problem. I told Rafe that all they did was talk, but he said I didn't understand. It hurt my feelings, but then he explained. The assay office is where all the miners, including Rafe, keep their ore until the monthly trip off the mountain. Even though there are iron bars on the window and a strongbox, Rafe fears that won't be enough to keep out the Stockton gang. He said he is also worried about my safety. He is going to propose that the town hire a sheriff. He kissed me again and I didn't want him to stop. It seems like I'm waiting for my life to begin. I pray every night for God to clear the way for us to be together.

# FOURTEEN

"As much as I hate to admit it, Phil, I'm glad you're here." Tom sipped the hot coffee Leigh had poured for him. With crutches, he was able to negotiate fairly well but he couldn't climb stairs, so he had spent the night in the easy chair covered with Gran's thickest quilts. Now he had kinks and creaks — more than usual for a man of fifty.

Phil grunted and focused on his own coffee. Tom could see the signs of little sleep. It gave him a moment of perverse pleasure to know that his brother-in-law hadn't slept well. He deserved it after what he had put Leigh through. Then Tom thought back to that moment on the mountain. In that split second when he was going to slide off the rock shelf and plunge into the ravine, it had been Phil's hand that reached for him. It had been Phil — the man who had broken his kid sister's heart who'd saved his life.

It was a sobering thought.

Tom's anger evaporated. He couldn't judge Phillip — he had his own sins to account for. There had been a time when he would've taken all his worries to God in prayer. But after Rose left, he had stopped praying. He didn't talk to God anymore. It was too painful.

He set the coffee cup on the table and grimaced. Just as Phil had the classic, textbook mid-life crisis, Tom admitted — to himself at least — that he was having a classic crisis of faith. He understood it, but he didn't know how to fix it.

That was why he had taken Leigh up on the invitation. Of course he was worried about her, and angry about what Phillip had done, but if truth were told, he had come here to Gran's house in the hope that he would regain his wonder for living. He'd hoped that he would feel God's hand on his head and His love in his heart.

Tom missed the Lord and wanted that passion of faith back in his broken, lonely life.

"Scrambled or fried?" Leigh's voice shook Tom from his own thoughts. She turned the strips of bacon she was frying.

"Scrambled is great. Besides, as I recall, you always break the yoke anyway, I might as well order them scrambled from the start."

Leigh grinned at him and he pictured her at twelve, all long, coltish legs and toothy smile. She was pretty then and she was beautiful now. There was a softness about her, a womanliness that only came with age and grace.

He hoped Phillip was man enough to see it and appreciate it.

"So, kiddo, tell me what you're doing to solve the riddle of the journal?" Tom shifted his cast and watched as she went about cooking breakfast. Phillip was nowhere to be seen.

"Well, we have some clues. Let's see, the first is knowing that the journal was written in 1859 and 1860. I'm trying to organize the church records, but with the boys here I wasn't getting much done."

"I could help with that. Obviously I'm not going to be moving too fast. I'd like to help."

"That would be great, Tom. Okay, so our next clue is the initials. Viv is still working on it, but so far she hasn't found anything. I'm intrigued by the flower and the teardrop glass."

"What teardrop glass?" Tom inhaled when Leigh put a plate of fluffy eggs and crispy smoked bacon before him.

"The author, Carrie, was given a piece of hand-fashioned glass, blue-gray, in the shape of a teardrop. She put a ribbon through it and wore it around her neck. Isn't that romantic?"

"Yes, yes, it is." Tom was distracted. Something about the description of that sparked a faint memory in his mind. He took a bite of his breakfast and tried to grab hold of the memory. Leigh had washed the dishes and he was on his second cup of coffee when Leigh sat down at the table.

"Okay, Tom, tell me what you think."

"About what?" He never really sorted it out.

"You know very well I mean Phillip and me — what do you think?"

He looked into his little sister's eyes. No matter how old and doddery they both became, she would always be his baby sister. He took a deep breath and tried to organize his thoughts. What did he think? What did he have a right to think?

"First I've got to tell you I'm mad — furious with him for what he did."

Leigh's face pinched with worry.

"But I don't have the right to be angry. I ruined my own marriage, so I'm not sin-free. How can I judge Phil? And the most important thing is whether or not you and he can be happy."

Leigh nodded and tears welled in her eyes.

"And of course, there is the other thing," Tom continued, with his eyes narrowed.

"The other thing?"

"What he did on the mountain was an incredibly brave thing to do. Phil is flawed just like the rest of us. But he has a good heart. I guess what I'm saying is that I love you. I trust your judgment, and even if I didn't, you're a grown woman, more than capable of making your own decisions. I'll support you no matter what you decide. I just want to see you happy."

"Thanks, Tom. Thanks for being you."

Phillip stood in the middle of the church and stared at the window propped in front of the pulpit. Arrangements were being made to chip away the plaster on the inside of the wall and re-install it where it had once been.

The light in the church glinted on the bits of glass. The scene depicted was lively, so real that it jogged something in Phil's mind.

"I've seen that place before," he mused. It was so like — no, there were differences but it was similar to a place . . . The scatter of flowers was certainly thicker, the mouth of the cave larger and deeper, but it was a real place; he was sure of it.

"Where have I seen that place?" he mused.

The image of the window had been in the back of his mind since Leigh unwrapped it. It had plagued him all night, intruded on his sleep. Of course he hadn't been sleeping all that well. Leigh was foremost in his thoughts. He loved her. He wanted to prove himself to her.

"I'm not a patient man," he mumbled.

He fought against it each day. He fought against the impatient fever to have Leigh back in his life. But he realized demonstrating his impatience would have the opposite effect to the one he craved. If he pushed her to give what she wasn't ready to give, then he could lose it all.

"Phil?" Leigh's voice startled him. He turned to see her there, silhouetted in the doorway. "What are you doing?"

"I was looking at the stained glass window." He met her halfway up the aisle. She was dressed in jeans and a sweatshirt. Her hair was pulled up loosely and his hands itched to take the fuzzy thing out of her hair.

"You left before breakfast. Tom and I had no idea what had happened to you."

"How is Tom?" And he wasn't asking about Tom's ankle.

Leigh studied his face for a moment. He could see the understanding in her eyes. She knew him so well. It was a powerful feeling — to have lived with someone until they knew your every thought.

"Tom wants me to be happy. He also said you were a hero for what you did up on the mountain."

Phillip hoped his face didn't reveal his surprise. He had never expected Tom to be so — forgiving. But he knew Leigh as well as she knew him, and he could see reservation, fear and pain in her eyes.

Only God knew if she could forgive him enough so they could try again.

That evening Tom, Leigh and Phillip went over the church records. Tom had them sorted by order of date.

"Oh, here is another entry written by Gus Reynolds. He has recorded a mining accident."

"That must be the one mentioned in the journal," Tom said.

When Leigh looked at him in surprise he grinned and said, "I used my time today to read to the point where your bookmark is. I wanted to be up to speed."

"So where are we?" Leigh asked. "Does anybody have any new thoughts?"

"Why don't you read more of the journal while I put on a pot of coffee. That would be perfect to go with the cherry pie I bought at Shirley's bakery." Phil rose from his chair and went into the kitchen. He was restless tonight. No matter how he tried, he couldn't push the image of the stained glass window from his mind. There was something — something about it . . .

He heard Leigh laugh and his heart tripped a little. She was the center of his world. In some ways he knew it was selfish of him to try and revive their marriage, but he knew he had to do it. Not only because he loved her but because he felt it was scriptural. She was his wife and he believed God wanted them to mend their wounds and stay together.

He said a silent prayer as he assembled the coffee and pie slices on a tray and returned to the living room. Then once again Leigh made herself comfortable and read.

*May 21, 1860*

The Stocktons hit Ironton just over the pass from us. Seven men were injured and one was killed dead. Everyone is worried. It does Mama no good. She is coughing again. Papa sent word with Mr. Gruber to the doctor that he will be bringing Mama in to see him next month. Rafe has been smiling a lot in spite of our worries about the Stockton gang. I wonder why.

*June 1, 1860*

The men have formed a formal city council. They let Rafe join because he owns property. Some of the other miners were excluded because all they own are their claims. I didn't know Rafe had been buying land but he has. Papa said Rafe owns two lots and is ordering supplies to start a house. I wonder if it is for us. I'm going to meet Rafe tonight after church services. We're going to talk to Pastor Johnson. I'm so happy and excited. I would like to talk to Mama about this, but she is still too weak and Papa doesn't have any time to listen to me because he is so worried about her.

"Now we have another clue. The man, this Rafe, bought property. Wouldn't the county recording office have a record of that?" Tom asked.

"You know, I think you're right. But we can't do anything without a last name. Maybe we'll find it in some of these records."

"Or maybe that is why the pages were cut out of the journal in the first place,"

Leigh said.

"You didn't tell me about that." Phillip frowned.

"Didn't I? There are some pages missing. I wondered why someone would do that, but now I wonder if it all has something to do with the missing treasure of Tear Lake."

"What are you saying? Do you think some member of our family was involved in robbing the town they helped found?" Tom shifted his cast and frowned at Leigh.

"Don't do that — don't give me the big-brother glare." Leigh shook her head. "I'm not ten anymore and I'm not intimidated. Now think about it. We have a journal that is old as the hills, it has initials on the cover that nobody can find a body for, and the only pages that apparently contained the name of the man this ancestor was involved with have been ripped out. What else could it be?"

"I don't know, but it has to be something else. I refuse to believe we're descended from somebody involved with a crook."

Phillip laughed and got up to refill their coffee mugs. "I heard of two spinster women who started researching their genealogy but quit when they found an ancestor who had stolen a horse and was summarily dealt with at the end of a rope. They stopped cold, put up some old portraits and made up a history they liked."

"That's it!" Tom snapped his fingers and scared Leigh so bad she sloshed coffee onto the old braided rug. "That is what I've been trying to remember."

"What?" Leigh got a tissue and dabbed at the spill.

"Do you still have that portrait done of Gran when she was sixteen? You know, the one with the fluffy hair?"

"Yes, I have it — it is at the house in the city. And it is called a Gibson Girl hairdo, Tom."

"Whatever. Can you get it?"

"The portrait?" Phil pulled a face. "You want her to go get the portrait?"

"Yes. It is important." Tom glared at Phil.

Leigh watched them face off like a pair of angry dogs. Then she got a little annoyed herself. Right now Phillip had no right to question anything she did. He had thrown that right away.

"Sure, I'll go get it," Leigh said. "I'll go first thing in the morning."

"Good. And do you still have that little cedar jewelry box of Gran's?" Tom's eyes were bright with some information that only he possessed — some secret he wasn't ready to share.

"Yes, I've got it. Is there anything else you want?" Leigh laughed. It had been a long while since she'd seen Tom so animated and interested. The divorce had kind of washed away his enthusiasm for life. It was good to see the old Tom again.

"No, that's all for now. But if I think of anything, I'll call you."

Phil got up and went into the kitchen. Leigh picked up her empty mug along with Tom's and followed him. He was rinsing his mug at the sink. His back was to her but she could read the tension in the line of his shoulders.

"Are you thinking of going by yourself?" Phil's voice was soft.

For a moment Leigh almost said no; she almost asked him to come along. Then she thought of Tom here on his own. "Yes, I am. Besides, Tom may need hclp. And I may decide to bring a few more things from the house."

"So you have decided you're not coming . . . home?"

"Home is where the heart is, Phillip. And right now my home is here in Tear Lake."

That night the atmosphere in Gran's house was tense and quiet when Leigh opened the journal and started to read. Tom closed his eyes and never made a sound. Phillip stared into the flames as if he were trying to see through to tomorrow.

*May 30, 1860*

Rafe and I have been speaking with Pastor Johnson. He has suggested a way we can be together if we dare. I am not sure. I don't want to hurt Mama and Papa, but I am so in love. The pastor says we should not worry, that it will all be fine in the end. He assures me my parents will forgive us. But I am unsure. What if we make a horrible mistake?

# Fifteen

Phillip watched the small pickup swing out onto the road. At least Leigh had taken the truck after he insisted it was both of theirs and she should use it. In the end he thought she only accepted because she would be able to haul back anything she might decide to bring.

"If only I could show her I'm a different man," he muttered.

"Talking to yourself, huh?" Tom clattered out on the porch and flopped into a wicker chair. He set his crutches aside. His voice was gruff, but there was a glint of humor in his eyes. Dressed in a faded black buffalo-plaid shirt and khaki pants with one scuffed brogan on his cast-free foot, he didn't look very intimidating. Clancy trailed behind him. He yawned and flopped down, clearly dejected at being left behind.

Phil shared his sorrow. He wrapped his fingers around the coffee cup he held and tried to absorb its warmth, but the chill of guilt and the loss of Leigh remained.

"I miss her so much, you know? Here in the house together but with a million hurts between us, it is almost worse than when I was staying at the motel," Phil said honestly. "There is a time in the mornings, when it is still dark, that I miss her the most. Years ago — before . . . before I ruined things — I used to reach out and touch her shoulder and she would sort of purr, like a kitten. And when she first gets up in the morning her eyes are a little bit puffy and her hair is wild and tangled. She is adorable. Those are times I miss the most. Not when she's perfect, with her makeup on and her hair fixed. I wish I had realized her inner beauty before I . . . well, before."

Tom was staring into space. After a long pause he said, "Rose used to pull covers. It didn't matter if it was summertime and the house was hot, she would tug covers. One night I was sound asleep and she hauled on that sheet so hard that I flipped over. There we were, suddenly wide awake, staring into each other's eyes, nose to nose. It was hysterical." Tom laughed, but his joy was short-lived. A shadow flitted across his eyes.

"Look, Phil, a part of me hopes you can pull this off. If Leigh can forgive you after what you did, then maybe there is hope for a guy like me. I never cheated on Rose. I never looked at another woman, and I know in my heart I never would have, but I wasn't the husband I should have been. I guess one kind of hurt is just as bad as another. If I could have one wish in the world, I would wish to be Rose's Superman. If I could manage to do one super-human thing to impress her so she would look at me with admiration again . . . well, I would risk life and limb to do it."

Phil thought about Tom's words. Could that be it? Was that the secret? Did he need to find a way to win Leigh's admiration? If he could do something wonderful, then maybe it would be the first really solid step toward reconciliation. He had given up his car, not to impress Leigh but to feel better about himself — to do something unselfish.

There were no more dragons to slay. What could he do to make her see him as a hero again?

"Maybe you're right, Tom. Maybe I need to do what nobody else has been able to do for over a hundred years."

Phillip stood in the church alone. He had been here for an hour and after his initial greeting and welcome from Pastor Miller, the cleric had gone to his office. There was something about that stained glass window that Phillip couldn't put out of his mind. He was sure he had seen a place very much like it — but where? The mountain was dotted with little valleys.

"Oh, hello, Phillip." Shirley had entered the church and he hadn't even heard her. "I was going to call you later. I found another bit of information about the Stockton gang."

"Really? What?" Phil's heart skipped a beat. Maybe his idea wasn't just a hollow dream. Perhaps God was lending him a hand.

"There was a rumor around town that goes way back. Some people believe the reason the Stocktons were so successful for so long is because they had an inside man. There is nothing concrete, but an old newspaper clipping I found in Durango implied the gang would place someone in the town they were going to rob and have him become part of the fabric of life. They could get information and details that made their raids very efficient."

"An inside guy — is that all?" Shirley nodded. "I know it isn't much, and of course there was no mention of who it may have been, but I thought it was interesting."

"It is, and you never know. It may be just

the clue we need. Thanks, Shirley, I really appreciate you digging for us."

"No problem. I love a good mystery, and this one involves the whole town. I expect you and Leigh to keep Brian and me informed if you figure it out."

At lunch Phil fixed ham sandwiches for himself and Tom. He brought them and a jug of sun tea to the back deck. Tom was sunning himself with his leg propped up on the empty rocking chair. His eyes were closed, but Phil knew he was awake.

"I spoke to Shirley today — I don't know if you have met her — she is the chief cook and bottle washer for the local historical society and owns the bakery in town. She's been doing a little digging for us and found out something kind of interesting about the Stocktons."

Tom's eyes snapped open. "You have my attention."

"She says the Stockton gang kept a mole in each town before they robbed it."

"And you're implying that inside man was a crooked relative?" Tom bristled at the idea. "No way, Phil. First, I don't believe this family was founded on stolen money or anything illegal. And second, if you were the inside man, would you then stay, raise a family, and put down roots? Uh-huh. You're barking up the wrong tree. The last journal entry Leigh read mentioned that man, Rafe, had bought property, so I doubt it is him either. If that story she told you is true, it is going to be a man who could show up and be welcomed instantly. He would have no ties, but would be somebody everyone would trust. He wouldn't be an immigrant and he wouldn't be courting a girl who had put down deep roots. He would vanish when the job was over. And when Leigh returns I think I can prove it."

Phil raised a brow to indicate he was doubtful, but he wasn't about to argue with Tom. This uneasy truce between them was something Phil didn't want to break. It certainly wouldn't help him to win Leigh back if he was openly feuding with her big brother. So he kept his opinions to himself and said, "Sandwich, Tom? Ham, cheese, onion, mustard?"

"Sounds revolting. I'll take two."

Leigh drove with the driver's window down. The fresh breeze whipped her hair and tugged at the collar of her blouse. She had the radio off and was alone with her thoughts. And, as usual, those thoughts were on Phil and the state of her marriage.

In some ways they seemed to be working things out, but she was still withholding a big part of her heart. Try as she might, she couldn't figure out how to change that. Every time it was on the tip of her tongue to bring up their problems and discuss them, she held back. She just couldn't do it. So nothing was settled. They had spent the last six weeks with each other, for the kids; now they were in the house together and she made the excuse it was for Tom's comfort. But the truth was she wasn't ready to be vulnerable again.

"I just don't trust him enough to risk myself," she muttered. Pastor Miller had said something the last time she counseled with him that got her thinking. He said that the amount of risk any person was willing to take with their emotions was in direct proportion to how much pain they thought they could endure.

"I don't think I can survive being hurt again," she said aloud.

And that was the nut and kernel of her dilemma. She loved her husband and believed that he loved her in spite of his terrible betrayal, but she wasn't yet willing to put it to the test and risk being hurt. It was as if she was standing on a cliff with a river rising all around her. She couldn't go back or she would drown, but she was afraid to take a leap that might bring her to solid ground.

She was surprised when she realized she was on her old street. She had driven on autopilot for the last 100 miles. It startled her when she realized she was pulling into her own driveway and didn't really remember the trip.

"I've got to make a decision about my marriage, and soon." She shoved her house key in the lock and went inside.

It was strange to be back in the house she had lived in for so long. Every curtain, cushion, window blind and knickknack had been her choice, but when she looked at them now they felt foreign and cold to her. She had hand-mixed every shade of paint and selected the carpet on the floor, but right now it seemed as if it were somebody else's house.

Was the house different or was she?

She thought of Gran's house, a mishmash of styles — nothing coordinated — and yet it exuded warmth. Or was that the residual happiness from all the people who had lived, loved and died in it? She wasn't sure, but she wanted to get what she came for and get back to Gran's house and Tear Lake.

Or was it Phil she wanted to return to?

She went upstairs to find the cedar jewelry box. Her bed was neatly made and bars of light seeped through the shades. The closet door hinge squeaked when she opened it. On tiptoe she felt the top shelf until her hands found the smooth wood of the little chest. She flipped open the lid and peered inside. The glitter of old costume jewelry and the patina of a couple of good silver rings that Gran had given her caught her eye. There wasn't much here, certainly nothing of any monetary value. But each piece was priceless with sentiment. Leigh couldn't imagine why Tom wanted it.

"Oh well, it is enough he wants it."

With the box under her arm she went into the spare bedroom done in old lace and pink cabbage roses. On the wall above the old French provincial bed the portrait of Gran resided. The mellow tones of an oval tiger maple frame complemented the soft pastels of the old oils of the painting. The twinkle in Gran's eyes was still bright and shone from the canvas. Leigh swallowed a hard lump that had formed in her throat as she came downstairs. She was nearly to the front door when she saw the red message light blinking on the phone in the library. She put the box and painting by the door and went to the machine. She punched the button.

"Phillip, it's me," the voice said. "I just wanted to talk to you and see if you really meant it when you said good-bye. Well . . . I was hoping . . . but I guess you aren't there, so — We had some good times, didn't we, Philly? Well — see you around. Bye."

Leigh hit the erase button. She didn't have to wonder who it was; the tone in the woman's voice said it all. Her heart ached with pain, but at the same time she was processing what the woman had said.

Phil had told the truth when he said it was over. He had ended the affair, or whatever had been between them, and he had come to Tear Lake in search of Leigh.

Tom was slouched in Gran's old easy chair with his foot on the hassock. He had turned all the clues over in his mind and he was confident his memory was correct. A small fire took the chill from the air. The room was warm and cozy. He should've been comfortable, but the company left a lot to be desired.

He glanced over at Phil, who had been pacing in front of the picture window in the dining room for the last hour. Tension radiated off him in dark, depressing waves. Tom had done the same thing for the first couple of months after Rose had left, so he understood what was driving the man.

Tom almost felt sorry for Phil — almost.

In his mind's eye he could picture Leigh pacing, worrying and waiting night after night while she waited for Phil to come home. So far he had not pummeled Phil, for Leigh's sake, but that didn't mean the thought wasn't always there in the back of his mind. Violence was no solution to anything; Tom knew that, believed that, but when he saw the pain in Leigh's eyes he still considered it.

A little voice in his head reminded him that Rose had left him and his marriage had been forever broken. Even though he realized it was hypocritical of him, he was bitterly angry with Phil for cheating on Leigh.

Clancy got up from his usual spot in front of the hearth and padded toward Phil. He sat down at a respectable distance and watched, his head swiveling back and forth like a spectator at a tennis match. Tom nearly laughed at them both. Abruptly Phil stopped pacing. Clancy dashed to the front door.

Leigh was home.

Both man and dog were tripping over themselves with joy. Tom considered himself a detached observer — he told himself he had no hidden agenda; all he cared about was Leigh's happiness. But truth to tell, it pained him a little to see the affection in her eyes when she opened the door and looked at Phil.

The bum didn't deserve her. Nobody was good enough for Leigh.

Phil was certain the house sighed in contentment when Leigh came through the door. He knew that he did. Phil wanted to hold her. He wanted to touch her. He wanted their life to be simple, loving and complete. The way it had been before. No, not like before — better. God was in Phil's life now, so it would be even sweeter.

"Hi, guys." Leigh put the cedar chest on the table beside Gran's overstuffed chair. Phil took the portrait from her hands. He smiled wistfully when he looked at it.

"She was quite a lady," he mused, lightly pressing his fingertips to the surface of the thick oil paint. It was touching. He was basically a good man; she knew that.

"Okay, Tom. Here are the things you wanted. Now spill it. What have you figured out?"

He wasn't listening. Tom owned a construction company. He had the hands of a craftsman. His fingers were long and strong, his palm wide, calloused and capable. Right now those hands were rummaging through the contents of Gran's old jewelry box like a hungry raccoon in a full rubbish bin.

"Give me a minute," he snapped. Then suddenly, "Here it is. I knew it. I knew it."

He held up his hand, and in his palm lay a small blue-gray bit of glass. A tiny hole was in the narrow end of the teardrop shape.

Leigh was speechless.

Phil whistled and said, "Would you look at that?" But he wasn't looking at Tom. He was staring intently at the painting. There, hung on a narrow ribbon, resting against the old-fashioned lace bodice of Gran's shirt, was the same blue-gray glass teardrop.

"It is the teardrop. Rafe made it for his lady love."

"Right. Our grandmother was wearing it when she was sixteen. I don't know who Rafe is or who CRT is, but I'm betting we're direct descendants." Tom held the bit of glass up in triumph and peered into its depths as if the answer lay inside.

*June 16, 1860*

Papa is making plans for Mama's trip to the doctor. Mr. Gruber is taking his big wagon and they are putting a cover over the back, and with the feather bed and all of our quilts, I know she will be fine. I'm praying hard each night she will get well soon.

*June 20, 1860*

Papa left today. Mama looked so small and frail among the mountain of quilts. Papa asked Rafe to check on me while they are gone. I'm happy he is beginning to warm to Rafe.

*June 20, 1860*

I'm hurrying to write this because I was sent word to meet Pastor Johnson in one hour. I hope nothing is amiss.

*June 20, 1860*

Oh, I'm so happy! Rafe got on one knee and proposed inside the church. Pastor Johnson was in on the deception. He asked about Papa, and God forgive me, I did not lie but I let him believe that Papa knew I wanted to marry Rafe. Well, in a way he does know and he has not forbidden me to marry him. I wish Mama wasn't sick so I could have had my parents' blessing. I know he will make a good husband. I pray I'll be a good wife.

*June 21, 1860*

My wedding day. I've a pretty dress that I was saving for something special and this is about as special a day as I can imagine. I'm wearing Mama's good tortoise shell combs in my hair. I'm meeting Rafe at the church, even though it is barely dawn. Then we're going to use Reverend Johnson's cabin. I'm nervous, but I'm so excited. It is wonderful to be in love.

*June 30, 1860*

I haven't written in a while and I take pen in hand as a new woman. How could I not be changed? Marriage is not what I expected, but it is wonderful. Rafe has decided we must keep it secret until my parents return and he can speak to Papa. I'm tired of meeting at Reverend Johnson's cabin and then coming home to my parents' house like an unmarried woman, but it will not be for long.

*July 1, 1860*

Rafe has hit a big vein of ore. He is happy, but he is also troubled by something. I wonder if he thinks I'm too young to share his problems. I need to find a way to show him I can be a helpmate.

*July 3, 1860*

Mr. Gruber returned without Mama and Papa. Mama must have an operation. The doctor has told Papa she should be fine after that, or so his letter said. I'm praying hard.

*July 5, 1860*

I've learned what is troubling Rafe. It seems several of the miners have hit big strikes. A lot of ore is being stored at the assay office. So far nobody has answered the town's advert for a sheriff. We're alone up here and vulnerable, with so much wealth. Rafe is jumpy as a cat but he has been working the mine, making glass and working on the new house. I married a good man.

# SIXTEEN

"Oh my gosh. She married him." Leigh set the journal aside. There were tears stinging the backs of her eyes. A hard lump formed in her throat. This marriage had taken place over a hundred years ago, but she was *invested.* Was it because her own marriage had disappointed her? Or was it because she still hoped for reconciliation?

"I don't know —" Phil said. "I'm not buying it."

"What? But she says so right here." Leigh jabbed the page with a ragged nail. The rough and tumble days with the inner-city kids had taken their toll. She wasn't the polished city dweller that she'd been only a few short weeks ago. For some reason that made her smile inside.

"No, no, I believe she got married; I don't buy Reverend Johnson's part in it. What kind of pastor encourages deceit?" Phil rubbed his temples. "I'm a young Christian, but I can't fathom any minister being involved with a young, virtuous woman doing something like that without at least informing her parents. No, it just doesn't sound right."

"He has a point." Tom eased his cast off the brown leather hassock and leaned near. "I don't remember seeing a single entry in the church records written by a Reverend Johnson. Isn't that a bit odd?"

Leigh frowned. Her sentimental elation about the wedding was evaporating under the scrutiny of her husband and brother.

"It is odd." She picked up a stack of yellowed paper and peered at it. There were holes, foxing and grime, but overall it was legible. "I don't think we would miss his name if it was here. The journal gives the date he arrived. You would think that the church entries from that point on would be in his hand, but they're not. We have Gus Reynolds's entries, and then it jumps up to March 1861. The first entry is about a funeral, I think." With a sigh she set them aside. "Now what?"

"We keep looking," Tom said. "Actually we should be feeling pretty good about all this. We have the little teardrop, we have the journal, and we have the church records. Three intelligent people should be able to do a lot with that."

"You're right. Maybe we should split up for a while — work independently." Phil rose from the floor and stretched his legs. He wasn't as young as he used to be and crouching on the old braided rug reminded him of that.

"Good idea. I'm going to call Viv and get a complete family tree if I can." Leigh reached for the cordless phone.

"I'll tackle the church records and see if I can get a timeline," Tom volunteered.

"I'm going to go talk with Shirley and look around a bit." Phil shook the pins and needles from his leg.

"Look around?" Leigh frowned at him. What was he going to be looking at? The clues were all here.

"I've a hunch and I need to follow up on it." Phil didn't want to give Leigh or Tom any ideas about what he was doing. Besides, a hero worked alone — didn't he?

Phil decided a cappuccino would kick start his little gray cells, so he walked into town to the coffee shop. His hands were shoved deep into his pockets, his mind divided between the old puzzle they were trying to unravel and Leigh.

His hiking boots thudded on the herringbone pattern of the street when he swung onto Main Street. The sun was glinting off polished brass knobs on the three-story Heritage Hotel. A scaffolding was hanging off the front while two men painted the ornate gingerbread fretwork along the roof peak. Across the street Shirley's bakery was sending mouthwatering scents into the air. The old opera house was alive with activity while aspiring actors lined up to audition for the summer production of *Our Town.*

"Hey, Phil, why don't you try out?" Walt Morgan sang out.

"No, thanks," Phil said with a friendly wave.

Farther down the street Bart Smith was brushing his draft horses. His old-fashioned buggy was polished and shined like a new penny. Tall, black wrought-iron street lamps had been painted and refitted with glass globes. Flower boxes spilled color from every street-facing window. Soon the town would swell with summer tourists.

Tear Lake was a popular destination for lovers of art and history. For whatever reason, the residents of Tear Lake had always been more interested in preservation than modernization. Now the town was a living woodcut of Victorian life. The streets, the buildings, the customs, harkened to a bygone age.

And at that moment, while Phil waved and spoke and greeted his neighbors, he was hit with the realization. He may have come here to try and salvage his marriage, but somewhere along the way he had become a part of it all. Tear Lake was in his blood now. He had put down roots — not too deep, but they were anchoring him to a place, a community and a woman in a way he had never been bound before.

Even early in their marriage he had not felt this sense of belonging. It was more than his love for Leigh, and it was more than the town. It was God working in his life. The Lord had changed him, opened his soul, and made him want to reach out to all mankind.

"And if I can solve the riddle, I hope I can do even more for Tear Lake," he told himself as he entered the coffee shop, inhaled the roasted bouquet of fresh ground beans and ordered himself a double dose of caffeine.

Meanwhile Leigh was sitting at the kitchen table with the phone cradled against her shoulder. The red gingham tablecloth was hidden under stacks of loose paper, binders and colored pens. She was scribbling notes in the binder and would occasionally draw a line and add a name on a roughly drawn family tree.

"Okay, so I've got Mom and Dad." She took a deep breath when the pang of loss hitched her breath. After all these years she still felt the raw ache of a child without parents. Death had come too soon to her life. Tom and Viv felt the same way, she was sure, but they had done their best to be strong and help Gran when three boisterous teenagers moved into her house.

"Right, I got Gran's name. And then her father . . . what was his name?" She halted in mid-letter. "That is a strange name. I don't remember ever hearing that before. Yes, I've got it, Thomas Trask Reynolds. I wonder where they got that?"

Leigh retraced the name once again. Her great-great-grandfather, Thomas Trask Reynolds.

"Got it, what is next?" She scribbled another name and then studied her family tree. "Gus and Emily Reynolds. Did they have any other kids?" She tapped her pen impatiently and listened to the rustle of papers on Viv's end of the phone.

Then her sister finally came back on and said, "Yes, one daughter, Caroline Rachel Reynolds."

"Caroline Rachel . . . Carrie. He called her Carrie. Oh, Viv, I think maybe you found her. The author of the journal was our great-great-grandfather's sister."

*July 6, 1860*

Rafe and the miners are meeting tonight. They are not meeting with the councilmen. I don't know why, but Rafe says there are good reasons. I got another letter from Papa. Mama is doing better but they will not be home for some time. We're still meeting at Pastor Johnson's cabin, but Rafe is not happy with that arrangement. He is upset that Papa is not going to be home. He says had he known this he would never have put me into such a position. He is worried about my reputation and Papa's reaction. He has said he may journey off the mountain to see Papa face to face. I love him. I know our marriage is not ideal, but I would not trade this happiness I have with him for anything.

*July 10, 1860*

The Stocktons are back. They hit the assay office of Red Mountain Camp last night. There was bloodshed and everyone is fearful they are headed our way. Rafe said something strange. He said there was some significance that our town was the only one not yet hit. He thinks they are waiting for something. But what?

*July 28, 1860*

Rafe and the miners have made a secret pact and not even I know what it is they are doing. I'm amazed at my husband's capacity to keep a secret. One wonderful thing, though. He has finished the gift for the town. Tomorrow after services he will reveal it to the church.

*July 29, 1860*

The gift to the town is a window. Each piece has been colored and shaped by Rafe's own hands. It is beautiful. When it is installed and the sun shines through it the church will be illuminated with a rainbow of light. I asked Rafe what the scene in the glass means but he only smiled. Now each time I glance at it I'll be trying to unravel the puzzle of the stained glass window.

*August 1, 1860*

Something horrible has happened. Pastor Johnson is missing. But Rafe and the miners are saying he left of his own free will. I cannot but think they know something the rest of us do not. I wish Papa would come home. I miss him and the town needs his level head, but Mama still cannot travel.

Phillip's boots slipped on a scatter of loose stone. He caught himself and continued upward. The path wasn't as easy as it had been when he and Leigh came up. In fact there were boulders and stones and obstacles everywhere.

"There must have been another rock slide," he told himself. The heavy rain had caused the soft dirt to give way. It altered the way the mountain looked. He scrambled up a ledge and stopped to get his breath and his bearings. He knew he was in the right place, but everything was different. Where a stand of aspens had been there was a scar of fresh, bare rock. It fanned out from a spot on the mountain high above his head.

"The spot I'm headed for."

Tom pinched the bridge of his nose and tilted his head until his neck bones cracked.

"Ah," he sighed in relief. He had been reading the church records for hours. His foot hurt, his back was tight and his eyes were blurring. Yet it felt good to be deeply involved with something.

"I'm not as young as I used to be. I think I need glasses."

Leigh brought in a tall glass of iced tea and placed it on the table near Gran's chair.

"Want some aspirin?"

"No."

"Then quit complaining. You're a healthy, vibrant fifty-year-old." She grinned and plopped down on the couch. "Have you found anything?"

"Nothing."

"All that reading and you found nothing?"

He sipped the sweet tea. "This could use some lemon."

"We're out, and quit trying to change the subject." She tucked her feet up under her and one brow arched. "Besides, grumpy does work for you. Now give. What have you found?"

"Okay, what if I told you the nothing I found is something."

"You're enjoying this, aren't you? Fine, I will play along." She settled back and watched him. "Tell me about the nothing."

"That is just it. There is nothing, no entry, no record of a birth, death or marriage for the entire time that the journal tells us Pastor Johnson was leading the flock here in Tear Lake."

"How can that be?"

"I don't know. I can't believe a churchman would be so lax about keeping records. Let's face it, in that time period the church records and the assayer's office were the two places most legal documentation was kept. What about that? Are there any records surviving from the assay office?"

"I don't know. It is in pretty good shape and besides the original jail, I think it is the most untouched of all the old buildings. I could go take a look if you think it might help."

"Hey, you think I might tag along?" Tom asked eagerly, levering himself up on his crutches. "I'm about to get cabin fever here."

"Sure, I think we can get you into my car. I just wish we would hear from Phil." She tried to keep her voice light and carefree. Her trust was growing, but when he was gone for long periods the old doubts crept into her mind again, undermining her confidence. And of course, since he never would carry a cell phone, she had no way to just ring him up and find out what he was doing.

"He must be onto a hot lead." Tom

grabbed his crutches and hobbled to the front door while Leigh snatched her keys off the hook and followed him out.

Phil used an awkward toe- and fingerhold to pull himself up. This giant molehill of rock had not been here when Tom broke his leg. Now it served as a natural barrier to keep Phil from his destination. He clawed his way up to the top and then paused. The sun was sitting low in the western sky. He had not calculated on all these obstacles. It had been his plan to reach the spot and return to Tear Lake before dark.

Now that wasn't going to happen.

"But I'm not turning back. Not now. Not when I'm this close."

The assay office had been built of rough-hewn logs the size and shape of railroad ties. Thick spikes of iron had been used in the place of conventional nails. The door was of a thickness and style that would've pleased a medieval warlord. One tiny window, no larger than a DVD case, was cut high up near the roof, which was constructed from four-inch-thick pine planks spiked into the walls every four inches.

"Built to last, wasn't it?" Leigh asked the blue-haired lady who sat behind the scarred desk. Tom clattered in and moved toward a glass case full of papers, ledgers and odd mining memorabilia.

"You're Mrs. Reynolds's granddaughter, aren't you?" The lady adjusted tiny gold-rimmed glasses and peered beyond Leigh to Tom. "And you're Thomas, aren't you?" There was an edge in her voice. "You skinned up my apple tree one year. I remember."

Tom grinned. "They weren't ripe yet. I remember too."

"Serves you right," she said grimly, but her eyes sparkled with humor. "What brings you here?"

"We have a question. Were any records ever stored here at the assay office?"

"Yes, they were." She rose from behind the desk and moved to a safe that Leigh had not noticed before. It was dark and practically disappeared within the deep shadow at the corner of the room.

"Some of the old property records were kept here." She pulled out a neat, modern ledger. "We have kept these because they contain the records of old mining claims. You know some of these are still valid under old Colorado mining laws?" She opened the ledger to reveal yellowed, foxed, molded sheets of paper that had been carefully conserved.

"The folder is acid-free paper, of course. And we have also had each page copied in case someone wants to do any research. These, of course, are too fragile to be touched."

"You mean you have photocopies we can look at?" Tom peered closely at the fragile paper.

"I can do better than that. You can check them out and take them home." She smiled and jabbed Tom in the ribs. "Just see you stay clear of my apple trees."

Phil squeezed through the crevice and hoisted himself up. He was finally here. His arms and legs ached, he was thirsty, and it was growing chilly in the shadow of the mountain. But then he forgot all his discomfort and stared in awe.

All around him was a carpet of white blooms. Just like in the stained glass window, they covered the ground and grew in abundance right up to the huge maw of a dark cave. The rain had changed the landscape completely. It had reopened the mouth of the cave.

"The cave in the stained glass window," Phil said.

*August 4, 1860*

The Stocktons are coming!

*August 7, 1860*

The town has fortified itself. Men are posted with guns and prearranged signals have been set up. I'm frightened, but I feel better since Rafe has let me shoot his gun. We set up targets behind Pastor Johnson's cabin. I started feeling poorly and Rafe went to fetch me a cup to get a drink from the well. He found something in the cabin — something bad. He wouldn't tell me what it was but he was in a hurry to get me home. He called a meeting of the miners.

*August 12, 1860*

Rafe and the miners have a plan, but once again I'm not allowed to know what it is. But I've a happy secret of my own. I wish Mama was here so I could talk with her, but I dare not write it in a letter until Papa and Rafe speak and Papa learns we were married by Pastor Johnson.

*August 13, 1860*

Rafe came in the night to tell me he will be gone for a few days. He says he is doing something for the miners. I'm worried.

Lord, I pray, please keep him safe. He kissed me and I nearly told him about the baby, but he looked so worried. I want to tell him when he is happy and not afraid for us. He said a strange thing when he left. He told me the stained glass window is more than it seems. He said I should always remember that.

*August 15, 1860*

The Stockton gang hit us last night. The assay office was their target, but something went wrong. Then we all learned the horrible truth. Pastor Johnson is one of them. He had been using us! He laughed at everyone, but he was angry when he and the rest of the gang rode through town shooting out windows. He said he knew there was a treasure in ore that was never kept in the assay office. He said he knew Rafe had a secret strike. He pistol-whipped one of the miners, but the man wouldn't tell. It was horrible. He shot all the men on the miners' council and then they rode out of town. I was so afraid. God forgive me, I was glad Rafe wasn't here to be killed. I'll be so glad when he returns.

*August 20, 1860*

Still no word of Rafe. There are whispers

in the town. I've heard speculation that Rafe was part of the gang, or that he took the treasure before the Stocktons got it. I know it isn't true, but I'm worried. Where can he be? He wouldn't leave me. I trust him with my heart.

*August 25, 1860*

Rafe's horse came to town last night. He was dirty, matted and hungry. Now I'm more than worried. A search party went out but they found nothing. In my heart I know that if Rafe could return to me he would have. Something dire has happened. My baby and I are alone. I know if there is breath in Rafe's body he will return to me. God, please watch over him.

# Seventeen

"I'm getting a little bit worried, Tom." Leigh stared out the window at the long shadows of late evening. The sun would set soon.

"He's a big boy, Leigh." Tom was using a magnifying glass to read the pages they had checked out from the assay office. He was completely absorbed. "Do you realize what this means?" He jabbed a finger at the little journal. "You do see the implications, don't you?"

"What?" Leigh hadn't really been listening. Her mind was elsewhere. Her heart was squeezed with fear. A man had gone missing more than a hundred years ago. Now Phil was somewhere — but where? Was the journal becoming a watery reflection of Leigh's own life?

"Leigh? Pay attention, please." Tom's voice was gruff. "Have you heard anything I said?"

"No."

He puffed out an annoyed sigh. "Okay, I'll try again. The journal says that Rafe found something in Pastor Johnson's house."

"I don't follow." Leigh rubbed her index finger between her brows. Her pulse was pounding in her ears and a headache was coming on.

"Rafe's marriage to Carrie was a sham. She was pregnant. Rafe found something in Johnson's cabin — I think he knew that Johnson was the inside man so he took the ore from the assay office and hid it." Tom's brows rose and he looked at Leigh expectantly.

And then it dawned on her. Of course, it wasn't so difficult to connect the dots.

"The window."

"Right, the window. He told her to remember the window was more than it seemed."

"It is the location to the treasure," Leigh whispered.

"I think so." Tom leaned back in his chair, grinning from ear to ear. "We have solved it, Li-Li. The Tear Lake mystery. We have done it."

"No, we haven't," she said. "We don't know where that location is. I wish Phil was here —" She stopped in mid-thought. Phil had been staring at the window a lot. Could he have figured it out?

Tom locked gazes with her. "You don't think?"

"I think Phil knew the window was a sort of map and went in search of the cave." She glanced out at the velvety darkness. "He is out on the mountain alone, Tom."

Tom's expression fell. He tried to cover it, but it was too late. She had seen the concern in his eyes. Better than anyone, Tom knew how dangerous the mountain could be after dark.

"Tom — what are we going to do?"

"We'll call Brian. He will know who to call to get a search going. But, Leigh — we can't do anything until morning."

Phil huddled deeper into his windbreaker. He had found some dried wood, and since he always carried a lighter, he had heat and light. But it was lonely. He was just inside the mouth of the cave and the wind moaned around his head like a banshee. A coyote had been yipping for more than an hour, and the swish and whoosh of an owl's wings whispered by from time to time as the bird hunted in the night.

But other than those wild creatures, he was alone. Alone with his thoughts and

God. He ignored his growling stomach and bent his head in prayer. It was a prayer of gratitude, a prayer of hope and thanksgiving.

"Because when the sun comes up I'm going deeper into this cave and find that treasure. Then I'll be Leigh's hero again."

Leigh and Tom were up long before the sun broke over the crown of the mountain. Thermoses of coffee had been prepared, blankets and a first-aid kit, as well as a portable stretcher, had been loaded on the ATVs that had gathered in front of Gran's house. Most of the men were seasoned professionals, grim and quiet as they prepared. The dog handler was a young woman who looked at Leigh with sympathy shining in her eyes.

"Don't worry, my dogs can track a cold trail in the rain. We're getting a good early start and the weather is perfect. They will find him."

"Thanks." Leigh hugged herself and rubbed her arms. She was chilled even though she had on a flannel shirt over her tee.

It was the chill of regret.

Because if anything had happened to Phil, she realized, regret would be her constant companion.

During the night two things had happened. She realized that she loved her husband, and given the choice of dealing with their problems and possibly being hurt or never seeing him again, she definitely preferred the former.

And then she had prayed to God, on her knees, with her heart and mind open, and she had been saved.

Now she wanted her husband back safe and sound so they could begin a new life together in Christ.

Phillip stamped his feet to warm them. His neck was stiff and he felt every aching bone in his body. But all in all, his night on the mountain hadn't been bad. Of course it was breaking summer and the temperatures had been slightly above normal.

He yawned and stretched, working the kinks out. Then he found a small pebble, wiped it clean on his shirt and popped it in his mouth. It was an old trick to keep the mouth moist when there was no water.

"I should've planned better," he murmured. He had brought no provisions and had told nobody where he was going. It had seemed like a good idea at the time, but now he was having serious doubts about his foolishness. Still, there was no reason to worry. He could explore the cave, see if he was right, and then head down the mountain. He would be back in Tear Lake before afternoon.

"Not a bad plan."

The sun was shooting warming rays into the mouth of the cave, turning the stygian darkness into a kaleidoscope of color. The walls were weepy. Tiny waterfalls spouted from the living rock and turned the stone green, brown and iridescent.

Phil moved deeper inside. It was still too dark at the back of the cave so he returned to his campfire and found a dry stick longer than his arm. Then he yanked out his handkerchief and wrapped it around the end and set it afire. It wouldn't last too long, but it would give him the light he needed.

He moved into the cool, damp cavern. There was a hollow, massive sound to his soft footfalls that sent chills skittering down his spine. Caves by their nature were spooky, but this one, only recently revealed after the recent rain, held a million secrets.

"But I'm only interested in one."

A strange sort of humming moan accompanied Phil while he went deeper into the chasm. He saw no signs of wildlife, not even bats overhead. Then as he rounded a sharp bend that bore all the traces of hard-rock mining, his breath stilled.

He stared in mute wonder.

A six-inch vein of dull gold and white quartz glittered overhead just above his torch.

"Gold."

Then his gaze shifted to a shape. It was a huge strongbox. The old-fashioned lock attested to its age. He moved nearer, excitement vibrating off him.

Then he halted.

There beside the box was a skeleton. The rotting clothes were obviously those of a male. In the bony fingers was a scrap of paper.

Phil eased it from the spectral hand and held his makeshift torch near. The words on the page made his heart ache. Then, with a sickening jolt, he realized what the vibration and hum inside the cave meant. He bolted toward the surface but a large chuck of the ceiling crashed down in front of him. He backed up, crouching low, taking shelter near the box.

A stinging blow to the back of his head made his world go dark.

"You call me as soon as you know anything."

Tom checked the cell phone for the tenth time. He wasn't happy he was having to stay behind, but there was no point in risking another injury. Besides, if Phil were hurt, Leigh wanted able-bodied men to help him.

"I will. You try not to worry." She hopped on the back of an ATV behind one of the men wearing a bright orange vest. Brian rolled up beside them on his own machine.

With a curt nod, the rescue leader started everyone off. The dog handler was way ahead, working the hounds alone, making everyone stay far back so the dust and other scents would not distract the dogs. Behind her were men on horseback and finally the brutish machines with the rescue supplies.

"Hang on," the man said. Leigh clutched at his shirt when the machine bucked and the wide knobby tires dug in, sending a rooster tail of dirt into the air.

*Please, Lord, let us find him,* Leigh prayed silently.

Tom hobbled up the steps of Gran's house and flopped down in the wicker chair. Clancy was in the backyard making his opinion of being left behind known to anyone within earshot.

"I feel the same way, Clancy," Tom yelled. He levered himself up and crutched his way inside. Clancy nearly bowled him over when he opened the back door. "Hey, fella, you and I are supposed to man the fort."

The dog looked less than convinced, but he padded into the living room, pressing his nose against the window. He whined low and mournfully.

Tom didn't blame him a bit.

He looked around the house for something — anything — to take his mind off Phil and Leigh. It had cut him to the quick to see the pain and worry in his baby sister's eyes. It hit him then, he might never really forgive Phil for hurting Leigh, but it didn't matter. God had, and Leigh had, so Tom just needed to stop judging his brother-in-law.

"And I will," he vowed. Leigh's happiness was the most important thing. He set his crutches aside and his gaze fell on the journal. They were almost at the end of it now. He picked it up and turned to the place where the little ribbon lay.

*August 27, 1860*

Papa and Mama are home. She looks the picture of health. Papa is so happy. He hugged me and asked me if I had been eating. He also said the Stocktons were gunned down in New Mexico. The man we all thought was a preacher wasn't anything of the kind. Everyone knows. Everyone will realize our marriage was not legal. But in my heart I know God understands. Yet, I'm lost. What can I do?

*August 28, 1860*

I must tell my parents. The name I had taken as my own is not truly mine. I was never married by a man of God. My child will be branded a bastard. Rafe is gone and I'm certain he is dead, because only death would have kept him from me. I cannot eat or sleep. I'm so tired.

*September 2, 1860*

I've told Papa and Mama. We all cried. Papa said I made a choice with my heart and that there was no evil in it. He blames the man who fooled us all into thinking he was a minister. Mama says my baby will come in March. She says I must eat more.

Tom's heart went out to the young woman. Those old times were harsh, and public opinion was unforgiving. Even though she and Rafe had thought they were married, he doubted it would have made much difference to the community. They would have been shunned. And knowing that Rafe never returned made her situation all the more poignant. He read on.

*October 5, 1860*

I went to church and met the new minister. He brought papers with him and the city council men sent a telegraph to make sure he is what he claims. He is nice. I cried through the service, not because of his words, but because to look at the stained glass window ripped at my heart. How many hours did Rafe work to make it? What is the secret it holds? Part of me doesn't really care. All I can think of is him.

*October 15, 1860*

I've taken to my bed. Nobody in town knows of my condition. Papa has told them all that I'm ill and must not leave the house. I pray my baby will be strong and look like Rafe.

*December 18, 1860*

I am so weary. My heart is not strong anymore. I live only for the baby. I feel like my life grew dim and faint when I lost Rafe. I cannot stop grieving for Rafe. I know it is not healthy, but he occupies my thoughts and dreams. I miss him too much to go on.

*January 7, 1861*

A new year. Another year without Rafe. Mama tries to get me to read the Bible but I cannot. I ache with the loss. I miss my husband.

*February 18, 1861*

The baby is going to come early. I'm anxious to see it and see if Rafe lives on. The child will not even have his name. I've asked Mama to raise it as her own. She tells me not to be silly. She says that I'll make a fine mother, but I know that is not true. I'm dying. I'll not see my child grow up. But at least I'll see Rafe soon. I am happy about that.

*February 22, 1861*

Rafe's son is born. He is beautiful. All dark hair and strong, lusty cries. I'm tired, but I'm content. A part of Rafe will live on. How I wish I could hear him call me Carrie once more. I'm tired now. I'll write more later.

But she didn't write any more. The journal just ended abruptly. Tom was sure it had ended with Carrie's death.

He swallowed the dry ache in his throat. It was hard to draw in breath. Knowing about this young woman and what she had suffered hurt him as much as if it happened yesterday.

Love was a hard thing sometimes.

# EIGHTEEN

"Over here! The hounds have found the trail!" The cry came up from somewhere within the thick cover of aspen and pines. Leigh swallowed her fears and craned her neck. She couldn't see anything beyond the cloud of dust being raised by the horse's hooves.

The rescue leader held up his hand to slow the progress of the ATVs. Her hopes sank. She wanted to push on, to hurry. To be moving and doing something.

"We don't want to interfere with the hounds, ma'am," he answered Leigh's unspoken question.

She tried to relax but it was impossible. Every nerve, every muscle was tense with listening, watching and waiting. Riding on the ATV had given her time to think, to imagine every horrible scenario that could happen. She thought of Tom and how easily he had been hurt in the rainstorm. But at least Phil had been there to help Tom.

Phil was alone.

Then she thought of God. He was with Phillip. That knowledge brought a peace and a comfort that amazed her. She was still worried and concerned but beneath those dire emotions was the assurance that the Lord would bring her and Phil through.

"His will be done," she said softly. And she meant that. No matter what happened, she knew it was all part of God's plan.

Phil came to with a bone-jarring start. There was a thick cottony feeling in his head and he didn't know where he was. He was on his face, and something hard was pressing against his cheek. He put his hands beneath him, palms against whatever it was, and tried to push himself up. A wave of searing pain along his lower back and hip accompanied the returning memory. He was prostrate on the cold rock floor of the cave. The back of his head throbbed and something sticky was in his eyes.

He opened his eyes, or at least he made the effort. One eye refused to cooperate. He swiped at the stickiness and realized with horror that it was his own blood. There was no way he could get to his feet, so he shoved against the floor and tried to roll over.

Agony licked up his leg, but he made it. Now he was staring at the cave ceiling. The sun was high outside and sent shafts of light into the damp hole, warming it. Phil looked around and saw the skeleton and the strongbox. And then he realized he was holding the paper.

It took a few minutes to focus but Phil was able to hold it near his good eye and read what had been scrawled there. The words were blurry but he could make them out.

"Last Will and Testament of Rafael Trask. I leave all my worldly goods to my wife and unborn child," Phil read. Then he squinted and made out the words written below.

> To my wife Carrie. I've loved you from the first moment I saw you. Take good care of our child. Yes, my love, I know. I had wanted you to tell me in your own good time, but for me time has run out. The miners and I agreed that I should hide the ore. They have taken a solemn vow to die before revealing it to the Stockton gang. Of course I had planned to return to Tear Lake, but I've broken my legs and cannot move. I set the horse free with the slim hope someone might find me. But that hope is now gone. Car-

rie, know when you feel the whisper of a summer's breeze, that is me. Know that I'll love you forever and will see you in heaven. This claim where I lie dying is the richest vein of gold I've ever seen. I leave it all to you and our child and those who will come after us. Our love is enough to last a lifetime.

Your husband, Rafe Trask.

There was something wrong with Phil's good eye. He blinked and rubbed at it. Then he realized it was the sting and burn of hot tears. The town's treasure had been kept safe; the miners had died with the secret.

"And now I may die too," Phil said to the skeleton and the silence of the cave.

"There must have been a mudslide in the last couple of weeks," Leigh overheard the rescue leader say conversationally to one of the other men. "I hope that guy wasn't stupid enough to go inside any caves for shelter. All this will be unstable until a new growth of grass takes root."

Leigh shivered. She was certain Tom was right and that Phil had gone looking for the cave in the stained glass window. She shut her eyes against the pain in her heart.

Once again she was struck by God's plan.

She felt small and insignificant when she realized that for weeks, her most pressing thought had been how to forgive Phil. Now her heart cried out for the chance to forgive him.

"Leigh?" Brian's voice ripped into her thoughts. "Leigh, would you like to pray?"

His words were like a lifeline. She nodded and took his hands. With her head bowed, she prayed to God above that Phil would be found and that she would be given the privilege of trying to make their marriage the solid, sheltering place it should have been for both of them.

"We ask this in the name of Jesus Christ, our Savior, Amen."

Phil shifted his weight and managed to pull himself a little nearer to the mouth of the cave. It was slow going, using only his elbows, but each time he moved his legs, a biting pain sucked his breath away and left him feeling nauseated.

He had broken something.

He glanced at the skeleton. The fractures of both legs were more than evident. It was a terrible way to die, but Rafael Trask had been at peace. He had left a message to his loved ones and made peace with God.

He glanced back to see that he had only

managed to get a yard closer to the mouth of the cave. He was exhausted. He had been foolish. The single bottle of water was gone, he had no cell phone and there was no nearby wood for a fire.

Phil felt in his pockets. Did he have paper and pen? If it came to it, he wanted Leigh to know how much he loved her, how sorry he was, and how he wanted to spend the rest of his life proving his love to her.

But he had God. And so he prayed.

"They have the scent again!" The baying of the hounds was like a heavenly chorus to Leigh. She jumped back on the ATV and hung on, this time leaning forward, urging more speed, more haste.

"Here, over here!" One of the men on horseback reined sharply and his horse scrambled up a scatter of rock and shale.

"We can't go any farther on the ATV," the driver in front of her said.

Her heart plummeted. "You don't mean we're turning back?"

"No, ma'am. We're going to pack the equipment and keep right on following those hounds. We'll find him."

"Thank you." She breathed again. "Thank you."

Within moments the efficient rescue team

had packed the necessary equipment on their backs and everyone was following the dogs and the horses. It was rough going and Leigh was amazed at how the landscape had changed since she and Phil had come up with Tom.

God was constantly rearranging the earth, she thought with awe. His mighty hand could move mountains, change rivers and repair broken lives.

"Give me your hand, Leigh." Brian stood at the top of the huge rock, reaching out to her.

She took his hand and let him pull her up, glad she had her sunglasses when the glare of the sun nearly blinded her. They had several hours of good daylight left.

"Please, Lord, let it be enough."

Phil must have dozed because he jerked awake with the awareness that a sound had intruded on his rest. He tilted his head and listened. He was about to give up when he heard it again.

It was a bark.

There were dogs on the mountain.

"Here! Help!" He cupped his hands around his mouth and yelled. He stared at the mouth of the cave, but his good eye was on the wrong side and he couldn't really focus well.

The sound of many dogs barking made his pulse race. Dogs. Lots of dogs.

"Rescue dogs," he said aloud. *"Help! Help!"*

The first one burst in like a black and tan bulldozer. The bloodhound's wrinkled face and soulful eyes were the most beautiful things Phil had ever seen.

"Hey, fella, tell me you're not alone." Phil tried to laugh, but it was a rusty broken squawk. More dogs barreled into the cave, sniffing, baying, barking, and filling the echoing chamber with the sounds of glorious life. Phil shut his good eye and allowed the sound to wash over him like a cresting wave.

"Are you Phillip?" a voice asked.

He opened his eye to see a group of people and horses, and then he saw her.

Leigh was crying and laughing as she ran past the men who parted to give her access. She fell to her knees and touched Phil's face with her gentle fingertips. His heart nearly burst with love and gratitude that he had been given this second chance. Emotion choked him, unshed tears blinded him, but it was all right. It was going to be all right.

"Leigh, darling. I thought — never mind what I thought. I've found it — the treasure and Rafe."

"Don't try to talk," she said.

A man started unloading emergency supplies. He put a blood pressure cuff on Phil's arm and began to poke him here and there.

"I want to talk. Leigh, I've got to ask you something."

The man was using a little flashlight to peer into Phil's eye. When he probed around the swollen one, a lick of hot pain radiated across his jaw line. Several of the rescue people had moved to Rafe's skeleton. They were discussing him in soft reverent tones.

Then someone noticed the vein of gold.

And the strongbox. There was a flurry of activity as the puzzle fell into place.

"Leigh," Phil began, but the man popped a thermometer in Phil's mouth. He was obliged to wait, the long seconds dragging on for an eternity. Finally the thermometer was removed.

"Leigh —" Once again he was prodded and checked. A collar was being put around his neck. It pushed against his jaw. Panic or something like it rose up inside. He had to know.

"Leigh," he yelled. "Will you marry me?"

The activity in the cave ceased. Even the snuffling dogs halted. Everyone seemed to be holding their breath just as he was, waiting for her answer.

"Yes, Phillip. I'll marry you again."

"Can I get you anything? Either of you?" Leigh asked Phil and Tom from the kitchen. They were resting in chairs with their legs elevated. Tom was nearly ready to get his cast off; Phil was going to be using a cane for some time.

The fracture in his pelvis wasn't one that could be treated with a cast, so he had to settle for time and patience.

Somehow Leigh didn't think he minded very much. Lately he seemed to be a very patient man. He had even agreed to wait to renew their vows until he was up and around.

"You're a hero, Phil," Tom said with a grin. Leigh came into the room and perched on the arm of Phil's chair. He slipped his arm around her waist, and she leaned her head down to touch his. They were happy.

"I'm just glad everyone knows the truth about Rafe and the missing ore. And you two now know the truth about your ancestry." Phil winked at Leigh.

"Yes, yes, we do." Tom was thoughtful. "So Carrie was our great-great-great-grandmother. Gus and his wife raised the boy as their own and the town never knew anything because of the illnesses. I still feel bad about Carrie never knowing what happened to Rafe, though."

"It is sad, but she never lost faith in him, that is what counts," Leigh said.

"So tell me, what are you two and Viv going to do with the mine?" Phil asked. After a few days of digging, Shirley and Brian had determined that Rafe's mining claim was legally the property of Leigh and her siblings. The journal and church records had proven it all.

"You three are rich as Midas."

"I was already rich," Leigh murmured. "I know what I'm going to do with my share," she said with a coy smile.

"What?"

"I'm going to give it to the town with the suggestion they erect a building for public use. And I'm going to ask them to name it the Caroline Rachel Reynolds Trask building."

# NINETEEN

The sounds of the wedding march wafted on the warm summer air. A hummingbird flitted in front of the bride, tempted by the lovely bouquet of white flowers she carried. She was being escorted down the aisle by her brother. At the altar her husband and groom — one and the same — waited. Her matron of honor was her daughter, newly arrived from England.

The pews were full of friends — Tear Lake family — and they shared in the couple's happiness and strength in the Lord. Six days ago Leigh had been baptized in this little church and God's love bound them all with invisible threads of happiness and belonging.

"Well, Li-Li, this is it, this is your last chance to bolt and run," Tom whispered as they slowly made their way forward. "You could slip out. I'll hold them off if you don't want to commit to the old ball-and-chain."

"Not a chance. I'm ready." She smiled beneath the half veil she wore. Her soft mauve dress came to mid-calf, the gossamer fabric swishing against her calves as she walked. Cassie had insisted she observe tradition and wear something old, new, borrowed and blue. The little blue-gray teardrop hung from a satin ribbon, and a lovely antique brooch from Cassie took care of the old and borrowed. Phil had given her a small chunk of gold set in a traditional ring mount to satisfy the new.

Phil's eyes lit with love when Tom put Leigh's hand in his. Was any bride more beautiful? He doubted it was possible.

So, with the sun sending rays of light through the stained glass window, Phil and Leigh vowed before God to be faithful and loving all the days of their lives.

## ABOUT THE AUTHOR

**Innis Grace** lives in northern New Mexico. She is well acquainted with towns that dot the Rocky Mountains. This is her first contemporary novel. As Linda Lea Castle she has written fourteen historical romances and is an award-winning, internationally renowned author. Her books are known to have history, mystery, faith and inspiration. You may e-mail her at: lindaleacastle@ptnet.com.

The employees of Thorndike Press hope you have enjoyed this Large Print book. All our Thorndike and Wheeler Large Print titles are designed for easy reading, and all our books are made to last. Other Thorndike Press Large Print books are available at your library, through selected bookstores, or directly from us.

For information about titles, please call:

(800) 223-1244

or visit our Web site at:

www.gale.com/thorndike
www.gale.com/wheeler

To share your comments, please write:

Publisher
Thorndike Press
295 Kennedy Memorial Drive
Waterville, ME 04901